REQUIEM

RICK MOFINA

REQUIEM
By Rick Mofina

Copyright © 2022 Rick Mofina

ISBN 978-1-77242-152-1

Carrick Publishing

Cover design by James T. Egan, bookflydesign

Also by Rick Mofina

This book is for

Wendy Dudley

Time as he grows old teaches us all things.

~ Aeschylus (525-456 B.C.)

PART ONE

CHAPTER 1

Mexico City and Los Angeles

Wanda Stroud gripped the armrests as the 737 accelerated down the runway at Mexico City's International Airport.

The fluttering in her stomach increased as the plane left the earth and climbed, the force pushing her into her seat. Taking deep breaths, she glanced out her window at the metropolis rolling below. The jet ascended higher and higher, until finally it leveled off. Relief washed over her.

Wanda might be a nervous flyer—*okay, I'm nervous about a lot of things since I lost Ed*—but she would not let it prevent her from traveling, especially since it concerned her medical condition. She'd hoped the specialists in Mexico would identify what she had and treat her, unlike the doctors in California.

She'd always been vigilant about her health, constantly checking for signs of illness. Always anxious about whether a sore throat or runny nose was an indication of something serious, then consulting her doctor to see if she needed immediate attention.

One night, a couple of months ago, Wanda had watched a TV program about a woman who had what was feared to be a new form of incurable cancer.

Convinced she had the symptoms, Wanda went to her doctor, who ran a number of tests.

"Your results are negative. You're fine," Dr. Singer said, smiling at her from behind her red-framed glasses.

But Wanda didn't believe that she was well. She went to a second doctor, who, after testing Wanda, agreed with the first doctor's findings; there was nothing wrong with Wanda's physical health.

Still, Wanda suspected the tests were incorrect, and that she'd been misdiagnosed. She feared that she had the new form of incurable cancer. So, she did what she often did—she went online to do her own research. At her own expense, she arranged to go to Mexico to see doctors there, who—according to the online chat groups—were close to finding breakthrough therapies for the cancer that Wanda was convinced she had.

After spending a small fortune and several weeks being examined in Mexico City—first at the renowned research center, then at the cancer institute—the results came back.

"The cancer you are concerned about is extremely rare, and, I assure you, you do not have it." Dr. Salazar of the University Center had removed his glasses, and looked at her with a measure of mild, but warm, exasperation. Then he gave her the same advice that her doctors in Los Angeles had given her.

"Mrs. Stroud," Dr. Salazar said, "when you return to Los Angeles, I suggest you consult your physician about relaxation techniques and refrain from online searches about your health. Your family doctor might recommend medication or therapy to help you with your anxiety and coping skills every time you think you experience a symptom."

Now, as the jetliner cruised 35,000 feet over the Sonoran Desert, Wanda settled into her new seat. She was late boarding because she had requested to move from her assigned seat, at the back of the plane, to one closer to the front, where she preferred to be. The flight was at 50% capacity, so the attendant moved her up

3

when the plane leveled. Wanda looked at the two vacant seats in her row, then to the seats near her. Most were empty, leaving her to take stock of her life.

It'd been five years since Ed, a city bus driver, clutched his chest in the grocery store, collapsed, and died in the deli section. Some days she swore she still heard him shaving in the bathroom, or making a sandwich in the kitchen. She was a 66-year-old retired librarian, a widow with no children, going home to an empty house, fearing she had an undetected illness.

She swallowed, and felt a tickle in her throat.

What was that? Did they miss something? Maybe I should see a new specialist in L.A.?

She turned to the window and sighed.

Maybe I should just stop acting like a foolish old woman.

Wanda then considered her paperback mystery novel. She decided to take her mind off of her worries, settle in, and resume reading.

That's when she looked at the lone passenger in the row in front of her—a man, in his 50s, with white hair, and working on his laptop. It had a big screen with a large font, giving Wanda a clear and inviting view over his shoulder. Being interested in what people read, Wanda decided to take a peek.

Just a little one.

Was he reading a book, or working on something business-related? She was curious.

Okay, so I'm nosy.

He had a few files open and was scrolling through them—photos of children.

His children? Grandchildren, nieces, nephews?

Smiling, Wanda thought, whoever they were, it was nice. She often wished she'd had children, but pushed the regret away. Reaching for her book, she thought again.

Wait.

She glanced back at the man's screen and the little faces flowing by. The children all appeared to be young.

Occasionally, he stopped the flow, which allowed Wanda to see how each child's face was framed exactly the same way. Focusing, she noticed that the bottom right corner of each photo was labeled with a multidigit number.

Like a catalog or gallery of children. Is it a school album?

The man's keyboard clicked as he typed, with Wanda reading his messages. Several terms and fragments of sentences emerged: *adoptee...agreement...transfer of rights to adoptive parents...will obtain a decree...facilitator...fees...will secure authentic-looking records and legal documents...validating legal status as an orphan...*

Wanda caught her breath.

Authentic-looking records? What does that mean?

The man's keyboard continued clicking as he continued what appeared to be a discussion with other parties.

Correct. This week, we have solid offers for #0247 from Madrid, #6796 from Melbourne, #0055 from Johannesburg, #2095 from Moscow, #8849 from Buenos Aires, #3716 from London, and #9902 from Toronto.

Wanda tried to make sense of what she was seeing, when the man typed, *Updating price list offerings now.*

Price list? What could that be?

His laptop flickered. The gallery of faces now showed a dollar figure in U.S. currency next to each catalog number. The numbers and young faces scrolled by: $185,000...$130,000...$155,000...

Wanda's skin tingled.

Something appeared to be very wrong—*illicit, even.*

Could that man in the seat in front of me be part of some sort of adoption ring?

She cast around for an answer. Finding none, she came to accept that there had to be some rational explanation for what the man was doing. Besides, it was none of Wanda's business.

She opened her book.

But she couldn't read as the man continued his work. Again, Wanda was drawn to the faces of the children—their digital names and price tags.

My God! What if something truly horrible is going on right in front of me, and I sat here and did nothing? How could I live with myself? What's the message about doing something if you see something? I have to do something.

Okay, Wanda thought, she could get evidence, report it and let someone expert in these things decide.

She reached into her bag, got her phone, and casually swiped through it while checking to ensure no one was watching. She silenced the snapshot shutter click on her phone, muted the video recording beep, and then began taking photos of the man's screen. Carefully, she zoomed in, taking crisp pictures, photo after photo, until she'd lost count. Then she switched to video mode, and recorded the man at work and the contents on his screen. She felt a tinge of embarrassment for invading his privacy.

This is probably nothing, but at least I'm doing something about it.

Suddenly the man stopped typing.

He turned his head slightly toward Wanda without looking at her.

Oh, no! Did he see my reflection on his screen?

He closed his laptop with a snap, and then raised his seat.

Wanda shoved her phone in her bag.

Oh God! He knows! He knows I've been watching him!

CHAPTER 2

Los Angeles, California

Wanda's heart beat faster.

She took up her book and forced herself to carry on as if nothing had happened. But she couldn't see the words on the page. Worry clouded her concentration; she struggled to remain calm.

Did the man in the row in front of her actually discover that she'd been recording the photos and conversations on his computer? No.

It had to be coincidence that he'd stopped working so abruptly.

But how can I be sure of that?

Wanda didn't know what to do.

Should I report him? Tell someone what I saw? But I'm not sure what I saw.

As minutes passed, the saliva in her mouth evaporated, and her throat turned to sandpaper. Glancing up at the overhead console, she pressed the call button. A moment later, an attendant appeared at Wanda's row.

"Yes?" the attendant said.

Wanda glanced ahead. She didn't know what to do. The man was reading a magazine, leaving her paralyzed with indecision.

"May I help you?" the attendant asked.

"Could I please have some water?"

"Certainly."

The attendant returned with a glass of water.

Sipping it refreshed Wanda, and she continued to feign reading while debating what to do.

What if she was completely wrong about what she'd seen?

What if she set something in motion that couldn't be reversed, by making an allegation that proved to be false but which had grown out of control?

What if she started something that could ruin this man's life?

I'm getting carried away. This is silly. I have to get a grip.

Wanda turned to her window, searched the clouds, and tried to relax, losing track of time. Before she knew it, the public address system was announcing their descent into Los Angeles.

∗∗∗

After a bumpy landing, the plane came to a stop at the gate.

Passengers unbuckled their seat belts, stood, made phone calls, stretched, and collected their belongings.

Wanda remained in her seat, watching the man. He slid his computer into its bag then, and stood with his back half turned to her. He reached up across the aisle, opened the overhead bin, and withdrew his black carry-on bag. Making a quick estimation, she thought him fairly good-looking, clean-cut; he wore jeans, and a white shirt under a navy jacket.

Placing the strap of his computer bag on his shoulder and shifting it to his side, he set his larger piece of luggage on the floor. Staying in the empty row across the aisle, he made eye contact with Wanda when she stood.

"Allow me." Smiling, the man gestured to the bin above her, clicked the latch, and opened the door. "I'll get your bag for you."

Wanda smiled back. "Thank you, but no. It's checked."

Wanting him to precede her because she was undecided about what—if anything—she was going to do, she nodded to the aisle.

He didn't move.

"After you," he said.

"You go, please. You have more to carry."

"No." He gestured for her to move forward. "Please, go ahead."

Someone had cleared his throat.

Wanda and the man turned to the unsmiling passengers waiting in line behind them. People wanted to get off the plane. Wanda conceded, and went first. The man followed her, and they joined the others ahead of them, shuffling out of the plane, and then along the jetway.

They'd disembarked at Terminal B, the Tom Bradley International Terminal, and followed the signs guiding them to U.S. Customs and Baggage Claim.

On the escalator descending to the lower level, Wanda passed under the massive U.S. flag and sign that greeted her with the words Welcome To The United States.

While disappointed with the outcome of her Mexico trip, it was good to be back in the country, Wanda thought. She moved along in the river of arriving passengers to the Customs and Border Protection area and held a measure of relief because she'd lost sight of the man on the plane.

Good.

She didn't want to think about him right now. She was tired. She just wanted to get her bag, hop into a cab, and get home. She needed a good night's sleep in her own bed. Then, if she still wanted to report what she'd seen on the plane, well…

I'll think about it later.

Walking through the terminal, unaware that the man was walking directly behind her, Wanda's thoughts shifted.

She hadn't been confident enough in her technical skills to use the mobile passport process on her phone, so she'd completed the blue customs declaration form on the plane. Withdrawing it now from her bag, along with her passport and airline ticket, she joined the long queue zigzagging toward the line of desks and CBP agents.

For the next 15 minutes, Wanda inched her way through the maze of posts and belts, and then caught her breath. *Oh no.* Coming to a turn, she suddenly found herself next to the man on the plane. There were a few other people, including a couple with two small children, separating them. But the configuration of the turn in the queue had put Wanda and the man nearly shoulder to shoulder, making it impossible for them not to notice each other.

"Hello again," he said, smiling.

"Hello," Wanda said.

"Quite an ordeal," he said, indicating the lines of people waiting to get to the desks and go through Customs. "Sometimes, this process can take a couple of hours; other times, you breeze through."

Wanda smiled and nodded, sensing that he wanted to talk, something she was reluctant to do. But their line was not moving.

She was trapped.

"You sat behind me on the flight, didn't you?" he said.

CHAPTER 3

Los Angeles, California

The man waited for Wanda to reply.

She hesitated for an awkward moment before smiling politely.

"Yes," she said, "I did. I was behind you."

He nodded, then said, "Mexico City's beautiful, isn't it?"

"Yes, it is."

"I was there on business. How about you?"

Wanda hesitated, glancing at the others in line. One man was reading a book, *One Hundred Years of Solitude*, using his declaration form and ticket as a bookmark; an older couple was talking softly in Spanish while tapping a map; and a young mother and father had lowered themselves to tend to their two toddlers, who seemed bored and on the brink of tantrums. No one was paying attention to Wanda and the man.

"Vacation," she lied, hoping the line would move.

The man smiled, nodding.

"Vacation," he repeated. "What's your line of work, if I may ask?"

"I'm actually retired. I was a librarian."

"Librarian?" His eyebrows climbed. "I love libraries. I do a lot research there. I write screenplays."

"Screenplays? For movies?" He'd awakened Wanda's interest, suddenly casting her anxiety in a positive light.

"Yes. In fact, that's why I was in Mexico City. Doing research for an upcoming project, a script for a major movie. A global crime thriller."

"Well, that sounds interesting."

"Brad Pitt and Meryl Streep have signed on."

"How exciting, I adore Meryl Streep."

"That could all change, of course. It's the nature of the business. But the producers want—actually, they demand—that the script ring as true as possible. That's why I was in Mexico, to research organized crime stuff."

"That's so interesting."

He nodded, while eyeing her closely. Then he lowered his voice, and said, "I wanted you to know, in case you glimpsed my research while I was working on the plane. I wouldn't want you to get the wrong impression." He laughed softly.

"Oh, no, well," Wanda's cheeks reddened. "Well, no, I—you have a very interesting job, that's for sure."

"It can be," he said. "It can also be extremely challenging."

A gap emerged in the line. Wanda gave the man a little wave before moving farther ahead, bringing their conversation to an end.

***

Twenty minutes later, Wanda cleared Customs.

She continued through the terminal toward the baggage claim area. Her unease about the man and what she'd seen on his laptop had dissipated.

Writing a screenplay. Researching a thriller movie. It all made sense.

She was glad she had never reported him, or made a scene.

He seems like a nice guy, and I would've looked like a fool.

She shook her head.

She had other things to deal with, like her medical situation. While walking, she reached into her bag for her phone and texted her friend, Colleen.

"Hey Coll. Just landed. Coffee tomorrow at our spot? 1? OK?"

Wanda would tell Colleen what the doctors in Mexico had said. Wanda felt that she needed to see another doctor in L.A. Colleen was her best friend, a sympathetic listener who understood everything she was going through ever since she'd lost Ed. She always gave her good advice.

Even though I don't always take it.

Waiting for Colleen's response, Wanda glanced around and saw the screenwriter again. He was near, but across the floor and a little behind her as they continued walking. He was on his phone. Wanda heard only bits of his conversation. He was talking in Spanish; she didn't understand what he was saying. He shot her a glance before turning away.

Working for Meryl Streep and Brad Pitt has to be stressful, she thought.

They arrived in the baggage claim area, and Wanda found the carousel for their flight. The conveyor system was humming; a few bags had emerged. While waiting with other passengers, Wanda's phone chimed with a notification.

Colleen had responded.

"YES to coffee tomorrow! Meet you there at 1! How did it go in Mexico?"

A parade of bags started on the carousel. Wanda glanced at it, watching for hers as she typed a response.

"Not so good. Tell you about it tomorrow."

"OK. Good flight?"

Wanda watched for her bag, and then went back to her phone.

"A weird thing happened on the plane. Tell you tomorrow."

"Arrgh! Don't leave me hanging!"

People had started collecting their bags when Wanda's large bag with the colorful flowered pattern appeared.

"Gotta go, sorry!!!"

"You're so mean! See you tomorrow!"

Wanda put her phone away and reached for her big bag, struggling to heft it from the conveyor, when the screenwriter materialized, and grasped it.

"I've got this for you," he grunted.

"Oh, thank you!"

"No problem." Setting it down, he took up her ID tag, and studied her address. "Wanda." He smiled. "I see you live in Downey."

"Yes."

"You won't believe it, but I live in Pico Rivera. Nearby."

"Really?"

"Really. What are the odds?"

"It's a small world, for sure." She smiled, and took up her bag. "Thanks again. Good luck with your script." She turned to start for the exit.

"Wanda, wait," he said. "The studio has sent a car for me. I can give you a lift home—no charge. It's on the way."

Wanda swallowed. Caught off guard by his generosity, she had to think fast.

"Thank you very much, but I don't want you to go to the trouble."

"It's no trouble. It's right on my way."

"No, really, thank you. It's very kind of you, but I've got a friend waiting," she lied. "Thank you."

Wanda started for the exit when she heard his phone ring. Walking away, she heard him drop his voice and start a conversation in Spanish, possibly hearing the word *flores*, which she knew meant flowers.

Outside, when Wanda made her way to the taxi pickup area, she sighed at yet another long line. Waiting her turn to be assigned a cab, she felt a bit ashamed.

Was I rude, too quick to refuse the screenwriter's kind offer?

14

It could've been fun to ride in a studio car. Maybe pick up some Hollywood gossip on what the stars are really like. Besides, if she had this new cancer, despite what the doctors told her, shouldn't she live life to the fullest?

"Wanda?"

Pulled from her thoughts, she looked just across the traffic lanes to a shiny, dark blue sedan that had stopped and was parked in a tow-away zone. The screenwriter had gotten out of the back seat and was approaching her.

"What happened? Did your friend stand you up?"

Her face reddened again as he stood near her.

"Yes, I'm afraid she had to cancel. Car trouble."

"My offer's still good. Come with me."

Wanda saw the car's trunk pop open, and the driver get out.

"I don't want to trouble you."

"Don't be silly."

"You're sure it's no trouble?"

"None at all. We're going your way."

"All right, then. Thank you."

"You know," he said, taking her bag and leading her to the car, "this is the same car Streep used, and she left her sunglasses."

"Really?"

"Want a souvenir?"

The driver nodded to Wanda, placed her bag in the trunk, and closed the lid. She got in the back beside the screenwriter, and buckled her belt.

"Thank you again," she said. "You really didn't have to do this."

"I know," he said, checking his phone. "But I wanted to."

As they pulled away and navigated from LAX toward the freeway, Wanda shivered with anticipation.

This will be fun. I'm glad I did this.

At that moment, as the car gathered speed, all of the door locks snapped.

CHAPTER 4

Downey, California

The next afternoon, Colleen Eden arrived at the coffee shop 10 minutes early and got a table by the window.

She held off ordering, preferring to wait until Wanda arrived.

Colleen wanted to hear about the trip to Mexico. Wanda was persevering, she thought, but Ed's death had changed her. It was as if she were a broken china cup that had been reassembled. The fracture lines were there—behind her smile, behind her eyes—prompting her to do impulsive things, like travel to Mexico.

Apart from grieving the death of her husband, Wanda had begun obsessing about her health, often imagining she had a range of serious medical conditions. Colleen had, long ago, gently suggested Wanda see a therapist about her unfounded health fears, but nothing came of it.

The best Colleen could do was be her friend.

"Hi. Can I get you something?" a man—in his 20s, with a beard, ponytail, apron, and rolled-up sleeves—asked.

"Thanks, but I'll wait 'til my friend gets here."

"Sure thing."

Colleen looked out the window, searching the sidewalk. Then she checked the time on her phone: 1:19.

Wanda's late. That's not like her. She's punctual and conscientious. No messages, nothing. Biting her lip, Colleen sent her a text.

"I'm here at our favorite table. What's up?"

Waiting for a response, Colleen thought back to when they met years ago at a CLA conference. At the time, Colleen was a librarian in Whittier and Wanda a librarian here in Downey, after working a short time in the records department for the Downey police. Colleen and Wanda had been pals a long time, and had been through a lot together. Wanda had helped her survive her divorce. But Colleen refused to dwell on the wound left by her adulterous ex.

She glanced at her phone.

My goodness.

It was now 1:35, and not a word from Wanda.

This isn't like her.

Colleen called her, but it went to Wanda's voice mail. She left a message.

Then Colleen looked up and down the street, thinking there had to be a simple explanation for why Wanda hadn't shown up yet. Colleen waited. And waited. But after nearly an hour, she'd become antsy.

What's keeping her?

Wanda's house wasn't far. She texted her again, this time to say she was coming over.

To be safe, before leaving, she called her again. Again, it went to voice mail. Colleen sent a new message, saying she was on her way. She left the coffee shop, got into her car, and drove.

***

Stopped at a red light, Colleen looked at her phone in her open bag on the passenger seat. Not a word from Wanda. Colleen couldn't remember a time when she'd been this late, or missed one of their dates.

What could be keeping her?

It didn't take long before she turned onto De Palma. After a few blocks, she stopped in front of Wanda's neat-as-a-pin yellow stucco bungalow, with the palms in the front yard. Wanda's Ford Fusion was in the carport.

Colleen rang the bell and listened.

Expecting to hear movement, Colleen heard nothing.

She pressed the doorbell a second time.

The house was silent.

She knocked, hard.

Nothing.

Concern pinging at her, she walked around the house to the rear, and knocked on the patio doors.

No response.

Shielding her eyes, Colleen drew her face to the glass.

"Wanda! Wanda, it's Colleen!"

Silence.

"She's not home."

Catching her breath, Colleen turned to see a man watching from the fence dividing the yards. Then she sighed. It was Wanda's neighbor, Len Peterson, the retired accountant and Navy veteran, in his backyard, tending to his thriving lemon trees.

"Hi, Len."

"Hi, Colleen. Yeah, Wanda's not home."

"Not home? But she got into LAX yesterday. She was texting me. We had a date for coffee over an hour ago, and she didn't show up. That's why I'm here."

"Odd." Peterson scratched his head. "I have her mail on my kitchen counter. She would've collected it by now. No lights came on last night. There's no sign of her."

Worry coiled up Colleen's spine.

"I don't like this. Len, I know where she hides her spare key. I'll get it, but will you come inside with me to check on her?"

"You want to go inside?"

"Yes, she could've been jet-lagged, fallen asleep, fell in the tub, or took too much medication. Who knows."

"Sure. I'll be right there."

Colleen got the key from under the egg-shaped rock in the flower bed near the window of the garden shed.

Wanda knew where Colleen kept her key, too. They had made a promise to look out for each other.

Len showed up with a Louisville Slugger in his hand.

Colleen looked at the bat, then at Len.

"In case there's trouble," he said, shrugging. "You never know."

They entered from the side door. The air was a bit stale, with a fragrant hint of cleaner, as they entered the kitchen. With its white cabinets and ivory backsplash, it was spotless, immaculate.

Colleen called to her friend.

"Wanda? It's Colleen and Len. Are you all right, honey?"

They heard nothing.

Len opened the fridge; it was bare, save for condiments, and jars of olives and pickles. Colleen looked in the trash; it was empty.

"Wanda?"

The small dining room, with its oak table and chairs, was empty. The living room was empty. The bed was made in Wanda's bedroom. It was empty. Her other bedrooms were empty. So were the bathrooms. No signs of luggage, unpacking, or laundry

The house held an eerie stillness.

"I've got a very bad feeling," Colleen said.

CHAPTER 5

Manhattan, New York City

"This could cost me my job," FBI Special Agent Jill McDade said.

Ray Wyatt nodded.

From their table in Bryant Park, McDade and Wyatt, a reporter for True Signal News, watched the children laughing on the carousel and the jugglers nearby.

With its promenades bordering the lush green lawn, the fountain, the gardens, the vendors, and café-like tables under the shade trees, the park was an oasis in the Midtown canyon of towering glass and steel between 41st and 42nd streets.

McDade liked the calm and peace of Bryant Park, and thought it best to meet there.

Her hands rested on her tablet.

"We've been through a lot together, Ray."

"We have."

"And I trust you."

Wyatt nodded.

"I'm going to show this to you because of what's at stake for you, and because I need you to see it, to help the investigation."

"Understood."

She tapped on her tablet, turned it to Wyatt, presenting him with a head-and-shoulder color photo of a boy.

As Wyatt stared at the image, the carousel music, the laughter, and traffic sounds faded. The boy looked lean, bordering on gaunt, offering a slight, nervous smile that pierced Wyatt, then ripped him open. Riveted to the image of the boy in the photo, a tsunami of emotions, memories, love, and agony overcame Wyatt, flooding him with hope.

Tears came to his eyes.

At the same time, he was terrified.

"I think—I think—this is Danny," Wyatt said.

"I think so, too. I needed your help identifying this boy."

"He's alive? Where? How did you get this?"

"Give me your word this stays confidential."

"Jill, this is—this could be my son!"

"I need your word, Ray."

"You said you trust me."

"Yes."

"Then trust me to do the right thing."

"Ray, this must stay with us. We've only just started the investigation."

It had been a few months since the Hydra case exploded in Vermont. The story had long disappeared from the headlines. Last night, McDade had come out to Queens to see Wyatt, telling him that maybe he was right to believe his son Danny was alive after all this time. But she was unable to say more. Wyatt had demanded to know if she was keeping information from him, until finally McDade asked him to meet her the next day in Bryant Park.

Now, here they were. After showing him the photo, McDade started elaborating, pulling him back through the years and the pain.

Danny was three when he was killed in a hotel fire in Banff, Alberta, Canada, while Wyatt and his wife, Lisa, were there on vacation. Canadian authorities told them how Danny had died with others in the blaze, and that they'd been unable to find Danny's remains—nothing, not even DNA—because Danny had been incinerated due to the intensity of the inferno.

Ray and Lisa never forgave themselves. Grappling with their guilt and grief, they'd refused to accept that Danny was dead. Ray had consulted experts who believed Danny's teeth should have survived, thereby enabling DNA testing and proof.

Without proof that Danny was dead, Wyatt and Lisa never gave up believing he was alive.

As time passed, Wyatt did all he could to search for a resolution. He pushed sources and reached out to people who were in Banff at the time of the fire.

Lisa went into therapy. Her psychologist had urged her to take up an activity to help her cope. Lisa found a pottery class at Queens College. A year after the fire, while driving home on the Long Island Expressway, a woman who was texting while driving crashed into Lisa.

Wyatt got to Lisa's hospital bed in time to hold her hand. He told her that he loved her before she said her last words to him: "Find Danny, Ray. Bring him home."

After Lisa's death, Wyatt never stopped looking for Danny. He continued appealing to other tourists who were in Banff at the time of the fire—sending messages around the world, begging for photos, videos, any recollection of the time that might help. People responded; they were kind. But Wyatt's efforts led nowhere until he received a video. It had been recorded after the fire by Italian tourists who'd captured a fleeting, heartbreaking glimpse of a boy in the townsite who looked like Danny.

Maybe it was Danny. Maybe it wasn't. But it gave Wyatt reason to believe that he could be alive somewhere in the world.

Now, he couldn't pull away from the photo of the boy on McDade's tablet.

"As you know," McDade said, "he'd be six now."

Blinking back tears, Wyatt's mind processed the stunning wonder of it.

"Why do you think this is Danny?" he asked.

"We worked with our forensic artists and age-progression experts. They told us that as we age, all human faces follow the same general pattern. Children in the same age group will often look the same," she said. "Going from age three up to six and seven, there is a loss of baby fat, the jaw gets a little fuller, the face broadens, and hereditary details sharpen."

Wyatt nodded without looking away from the picture.

"Our experts then analyzed all the photos you posted online of Danny, and the photos you've shared with me of Lisa and yourself. After applying cutting-edge computer software programs, they concluded with ninety percent certainty that this boy is Danny."

"Where is he now? Why don't you go get him?"

"I don't have all the answers. What I'll share with you is in the strictest confidence, and may be hard to hear."

"Tell me."

"I can't reveal much because it's part of an ongoing investigation that has only just been launched."

"I get that, Jill, but I deserve to know."

McDade glanced around at the park and skyscrapers, taking a moment for a deep breath.

"It arose out of Hydra, the man using the alias Lasius Byyle. The other man tied to the case was Devlin Foxe, the realtor. He had an online association with Byyle, and rented the property to him."

Wyatt nodded. "I know." He'd written about the case.

"Through his attorney, Foxe has been cooperating, telling us how he came to meet Byyle on the dark web. It gets complicated, very complicated, and it took us a lot of time to investigate. But members of some of their groups led us to tentacles of other groups, then others, and so on."

"What kind of groups, Jill? I know some people think the dark web is a haven for criminal activity."

"We suspect one is an illegal international adoption ring."

All the blood drained from Wyatt's face.

"Is that where you found Danny's picture?"

McDade nodded. "And photos of many other children."

"Are you going to rescue them? Make arrests?"

"We can't."

"Why not?"

"We don't know where they are, or who they are."

"I don't understand."

"Our people only got a glimpse inside this ring before risking being detected. It has extremely sophisticated security systems that require specific customized software. It'll take some time for us to infiltrate and get a lock on the players and their locations."

Wyatt stared at the photo.

Searching the eyes of the boy he believed was his son, Lisa's words echoed.

"Find Danny, Ray. Bring him home."

CHAPTER 6

Downey, California

From the poster, Wanda Stroud smiled at her friend, Colleen Eden.

It was a recent picture of Wanda, right there under the words *POLICE BULLETIN* and *MISSING PERSON*, emblazoned in bold red letters.

Next was a description with Wanda's date of birth, her height and weight, hair and eye color.

Then came details and dates—how Stroud's last known location was believed to have been LAX (Los Angeles International Airport) after she'd arrived in the U.S. on a flight from Mexico City, Mexico; how Stroud, a retired librarian, had texted a friend over the phone from the airport, planning to meet the friend near her home in Downey the next day; how Stroud failed to show up and had not been seen since. The poster offered a case number and invited anyone with information to call Downey Police or Detective Brandon Chambers.

At home, in front of her computer monitor, looking at Wanda's missing-person poster, Colleen's heart filled with fear. She found a measure of comfort in the fact she had called police and reported Wanda missing.

"You're doing the right thing," Detective Chambers had assured her.

She'd met with him at police headquarters after a patrol unit first checked Wanda's bungalow on De Palma, before setting the investigation in motion.

Colleen recalled how Chambers's eyebrows lifted slightly when she told him the now-disturbing detail of Wanda's last message from the airport.

"Something weird happened on the plane."

"Did she offer you details on what happened?" Chambers asked after he made note of the remark.

"No. None."

After asking her more questions about Wanda, Chambers assured Colleen that Wanda's case was a priority. He outlined all the police would do, including: contacting Wanda's carrier to track down her phone's location and the last calls made; checking all activity on her credit and banking cards; entering all the case information in all law enforcement databases and networks; and working with the LAPD, the FBI, and authorities at LAX, who could check security cameras.

"We'll issue a press release and get the poster up on all our social media accounts as soon as possible," Chambers said.

The Downey police had moved fast, Colleen thought.

Now, looking at Wanda's missing-person information, Colleen's thoughts raced with a million fears.

Praying for her friend, she couldn't stop Wanda's words from haunting her.

A weird thing happened on the plane.

CHAPTER 7

Alhambra, California

"Got anything for the Sked today?"

After reading the email, Sabrena Roha typed her response.

"Not today, Agnes. First day back."

Roha sipped some coffee, then contemplated the palms outside her apartment window on Almansor when she received a reply.

"No problem, Sabrena. Good work on the shooting series," said Anges Finney, the assignment editor with True Signal News in New York.

"Thanks," Roha said.

She scrolled through the Sked, a schedule of stories True Signal's journalists across the country and around the world were working on. The items were labeled with a single word, known as a *slug*. That was followed by a byline, identifying the reporter; then a placeline, identifying where the story originated; and then a short summary. Sometimes a story fell through, and it was removed from the Sked; sometimes it changed, and was reslugged. But usually, the articles came together.

Roha glanced at today's lineup. Among the Sked offerings were: JETMYSTERY, by Ana Ilano, MANILA: Families search for answers a year after jetliner disaster;

LOSTEMBRYOS, by Sylvia Parker, CHICAGO: Eggs and embryos lost after storage failure at fertility clinic; HOSTAGEHUNT, by Denis Hugo, PARIS: Dragnet across Europe for bank robbers who fled with three bank tellers.

They all looked strong.

Roha sipped more coffee, pondering ideas for a new story. She had just come back to work after completing a four-part series on a mass shooting in Los Angeles, and how it had devastated the families involved. Her heart went out to mothers, wives, fathers, husbands, children— everyone whose life was fractured by another senseless act. Writing on a tragedy was emotionally draining for Roha; it always had been. She was no rookie; she had done so many stories like it before.

You blink, and you've put in nearly two decades in this business.

Right out of college, Roha had parlayed weekend student work at the San Diego Bureau of the Associated Press into a full-time reporting job. In her five years with the AP in San Diego, she'd covered drug cartels, border issues, the military, sports, entertainment, and every tragedy imaginable.

Then she joined the *Los Angeles Times*, where she worked as an investigative reporter in Metro.

But the industry was changing. Newspapers were losing readers and ad revenue. There were job cuts. Scores of papers folded; many died a slow death. So, after 10 years at the *Times*, Roha took a buyout, figuring it was best before another round of layoffs. At the same time, she applied for a position with a new media outlet, True Signal News.

"Your work is first-rate," Chase Lockner, managing editor of True Signal, had said during her interview. "I like that you were with the Associated Press. My grandfather worked for the AP."

Lockner stressed that True Signal's mission was to get to the truth, no matter how long it took; to go beneath the surface of investigations; to break stories while striving for excellence.

"Sounds good to me," Roha said.

Lockner hired her.

Roha could work from home and travel anywhere a story required.

"Just give us good, meaningful reads, Sabrena," Lockner said.

She'd been with them for a few years and was glad she'd joined their staff. True Signal's subscribers now reached nearly three million around the globe.

All right. Time to find a new story.

Roha opened her folder of potential leads— unconfirmed tips she was pursuing. A regional car rental agency allegedly was obtaining vehicles from a car-theft network. An extremist group was plotting to carry out armored car heists to fund other operations. Somewhere in Calaveras, a cult, claiming to have made contact with aliens, was building a rocket ship to transport them to a distant planet to create a new world.

So far, none of her leads had gotten any traction.

Roha's focus shifted to a distinct, on-screen alert to an email.

She subscribed to dozens of law enforcement accounts that instantly informed her when a new press release had been issued.

This one was from Downey Police, a bulletin about a missing person.

Roha leaned closer to her monitor and read about Wanda Stroud, 66, a retired librarian, last seen at LAX after a return flight from Mexico City.

Roha studied the photo.

She looks like a nice lady.

Tapping her finger on her desk, she wondered.

This wasn't a Silver Alert. Nothing about a lost senior. Nothing about a medical condition. A flight from Mexico City? Could cartels be using seniors as mules? Could have nothing to do with Mexico, nothing to do with drugs. Could be anything.

Roha stopped tapping her finger and reached for her phone.

CHAPTER 8

Manhattan, New York

The diner was on West 23rd Street.

The counter had chrome-ringed stools, and there was a line of booths with green vinyl, patched with duct tape. It had a low ceiling, and the air held the aroma of deep-fried food, but Wyatt wasn't hungry.

His stomach was twisted in knots.

He went to an empty booth at the back, where he resumed analyzing what McDade had revealed to him the previous day in Bryant Park.

Danny had been stolen from us in the fire at Banff and taken into a criminal adoption ring.

Wyatt didn't get much sleep after his meeting with McDade. He could only think of the picture she'd shown him.

It was Danny.

Wyatt raised his fist to his mouth.

Danny.

McDade wouldn't let him copy the picture, but it was burned into his heart. It had ignited wild fears, because this FBI lead arose from the investigation of the Hydra Killer and was tied to a criminal adoption ring's networks on the dark web.

My God, what have they done to Danny?

Where is he now?

"What would you like?" asked a man with a white apron and a mop of dark hair standing at the table, order pad in hand.

"Just a coffee, thanks."

As the server left, a man entered the diner. Wearing a dark sport coat, white shirt, and jeans, he came straight to the booth, sighing as he sat across from Wyatt.

"Raymond. It's been a while."

"Thanks for meeting me, Tony."

"Getting back into the news racket has turned out well for you."

Wyatt looked at his friend and long-time source, Tony DeCastilla, retired NYPD detective, now a private investigator. He had offered Wyatt a job before True Signal News hired him.

"That was a helluva story in Vermont, Ray. From what I hear, it's going good for you. You got some book deal on the Hydra thing."

"The book's on hold. I don't think the story's ended."

DeCastilla detected something unsettled in Wyatt's eyes.

"What's going on? You seem uneasy."

"Something's come up. Tony, I need help. It's why I reached out."

The server brought Wyatt's coffee.

"Can I get you something?" he asked DeCastilla.

"Yeah. I'll have a coffee. Thanks."

The server left.

"What is it, Ray?"

Wyatt had weighed his decision before he sent a message to DeCastilla last night. He'd only promised McDade he'd do the right thing, and the right thing was to find Danny at any cost.

Now, at the diner, he related all he knew to DeCastilla, because he trusted him and because he needed help.

DeCastilla whistled softly.

"Geez, so the feds think your boy is alive with an illegal adoption network. Damn, that's a helluva thing, Ray, a helluva thing."

"So, can you find out what's going on with their investigation?"

"You want me to poke around in an ongoing FBI investigation?"

"I know I'm walking on a thin edge here. Maybe even crossing a line."

"No maybe about it, Ray. It's risky stuff."

"But it's my son," Wyatt said. "They've got to be working with people on the Hydra investigation. You must know some people with the other agencies on the task force who are on the inside."

"It's possible, but you've got McDade, Ray, so you're already further ahead than I could get you."

"She won't tell me much more."

"I hear you. She showed you the picture, to help her, and maybe because she considers you a friend. Not telling you more may not be nice, but you can bet she has her reasons—a big one being to protect the investigation."

"What about going to Devlin Foxe, who's cooperating with the FBI?"

DeCastilla shook his head.

"You know better, Ray. If Foxe is working with the FBI, as a key player trying to work a better sentencing deal, then going to him could be seen as obstruction. You gotta think this through. If you or I step into this, we risk damaging or blowing their investigation."

"I know how it works," Wyatt said. "There are police investigations, and there are journalistic investigations."

Wyatt rubbed his chin, picked up his phone, and scrolled to the last photos he had of Danny. They were taken at Banff. He came to a favorite—Lisa holding Danny, with the Rocky Mountains behind them.

Wyatt closed his eyes for a moment, feeling the heat of the fire, before opening them to the picture on his phone.

"Ray." DeCastilla saw what Wyatt was looking at. "I know this hurts."

"I've already lost so much. I've got nothing left."

"I know."

"Will you help me, Tony?"

DeCastilla looked at him, then nodded.

"I'll see what I can do."

CHAPTER 9

Alhambra, California

Roha's first call was to the Downey Police detective on the case.

"Chambers," he answered.

"Hi. Sabrena Roha. I'm a reporter with True Signal News, and I'm looking into the case of Wanda Stroud for a possible story. Do you have a moment?"

"Go ahead."

"This will be on the record, okay?"

"Sure. That's fine."

"Is she still missing?"

"Yes."

"Can you tell me more about the case, other than what's in the news release?"

"Such as?"

"Do you suspect foul play, or have any suspects? Is Wanda Stroud known to police? That kind of thing."

"I see." Chambers waited a moment. "I don't have a lot to share at this time, other than it appears she landed at LAX, called a friend, but never made it home to Downey from the airport."

"Any theories on what may have happened?"

"Nothing at this time, but it's too early to rule anything out."

"Your press release indicates she went missing after arriving at LAX on a flight from Mexico City. Can I get the airline and flight number?"

"Hold on."

The line went silent for several seconds before Chambers came back.

"It's a Mexican airline, Cee-ell-low-ah–our-rah."

"Cielo Ahora. That's Sky Now," Roha repeated, helping him with the correct pronunciation and translation.

"Thanks," Chambers said.

"No problem. And the flight number?"

"CA359."

"And given the connection to Mexico and LAX, are you working with other law enforcement agencies?"

"We are. Police at LAX, LAPD, L.A. County, Homeland, the FBI, everyone."

"What're they telling you?"

"Nothing I can share. But we're investigating with all available resources."

"Are they checking video at LAX?"

"That would be part of the investigation."

Roha took everything down before asking, "Anything strike you as unusual about this case?"

"It's unusual for her to go missing. Totally out of character."

"The friend she called from LAX that she'd planned to meet—is that friend the person who reported her missing?"

"Yes."

"Can you put me in touch with the friend?"

"Give me your contact info. I'll pass it to her, and let her decide."

Roha gave him her number and email, then said, "Is there anything you want to tell me? Anything that should go into the story?"

"I think that's pretty much it for now, except to say that we're doing all we can to locate her."

"Okay, thanks. Can I get the full spelling of your name?"

Chambers gave it to Roha, and then she ended the call.

For a long moment, she looked at the palms outside her apartment window, thinking how the call had not even touched the surface of the story, debating on whether to go further.

I'll dig a little more. Let's see what happens.

Roha opened her folder of contacts she'd developed over the years. She had hundreds of them. She also scrolled through others on her phone. She knew people with the airport police at LAX, Customs, Homeland, the Transportation Security Administration, known as the TSA, L.A. County, the LAPD, and the FBI. She also had sources within the Mexican Consulate in Los Angeles, and the FBI's legal attaché at the U.S. Embassy in Mexico City.

She got busy—sending emails, making calls, leaving messages.

She was getting up for more coffee when her phone rang.

"Hello," she said.

"Is this Sabrena Roha with True Signal News?"

"Yes."

"This is Colleen Eden, Wanda Stroud's friend. You wanted to talk to me?"

CHAPTER 10

Downey, California

Sabrena Roha drove a 2017 Grabber Blue Ford Mustang.

It had belonged to her fiancé, Cliff, a Los Angeles County sheriff's deputy, who was killed when he was shot in a traffic stop.

Losing him had turned Roha's world upside down, and became a factor in her decision to take a buyout from the *Times*. She withdrew socially. Worried friends tried to help her reconnect, but she never really got out much. She chose to focus on her job.

Still, not a day went by that she didn't think of Cliff.

It's been a couple of years. I've got to get on with my life. But it hurts.

She opened up the Mustang's V-8, heading west on 10, before south on 710 through East L.A., then continuing south on the Golden State Freeway.

Along the 20-minute drive, her phone vibrated and chimed with responses from the calls she'd put out. In keeping with the law, Roha used her phone's hands-free speaker and voice command features.

Most of her sources knew nothing of the case. One person left a message, but before Roha responded, the exit for Downey came up.

Colleen Eden had suggested they meet at the missing woman's house. Roha checked her GPS map, which guided her to De Palma. She came upon marked and unmarked police units, a media truck, and a dozen or so people gathered outside Wanda Stroud's bungalow.

The entire yard and driveway had been taped off.

She parked down the street and walked to the house, doing what she always did upon arriving at a scene: she kept her notebook in her bag and observed. She spotted a blue KTLA news van. A reporter holding a microphone, with a camera operator behind him, was interviewing a man. They used the yellow crime-scene tape and house as a backdrop.

The house was a well-kept stucco bungalow with healthy palms in the front yard. It was immaculate. A small Ford sedan was in the shade of the carport. A pretty place, Roha thought.

Inside the area taped off by police, masked and gloved members of a crime-scene team from the Los Angeles County Sheriff's Department moved between the house and their truck. Roha went around the vehicles, where she could be alone with a clear view, when a member of the crime-scene team, a woman walking to the unit's truck, noticed her at the tape.

"Sabrena?"

It took a moment for Roha to recognize the LASD forensic identification specialist who had been close to Cliff.

"Madison?" Sabrena said.

"Yeah, it's been a long time. How're you?"

"Good. You?"

"Working it, you know." Madison glanced around, then stepped closer to Roha. "So, are you reporting on this missing-person case?"

"I might be." She nodded to the truck. "Why're you guys here?"

Madison looked around again. She asked Roha, "What do you know?"

"Wanda Stroud, the woman who lives here, landed at LAX after returning from Mexico, and never made it home. Did you find her in there?"

Madison shook her head.

"I can't say much, but this is routine." Madison lowered her voice. "We're processing the house in case someone involved may have come here."

Roha nodded. Then, noticing the KTLA crew glancing their way, she immediately left Madison, and went to the TV team.

Roha didn't know them.

"So, guys, what's up here?" she asked.

The reporter, a man with well-coiffed blond hair and white teeth, let his eyes take a walk all over Roha.

"Who're you?" he asked.

"Sabrena Roha. I'm with True Signal News."

He nodded and grinned.

"Chuck Lancaster, KTLA. Just joined the station. Came down from the Bay. My partner here's a news photographer—J.J. Soledad."

"So, what's going on?" Roha asked. "What're you hearing?"

Lancaster shook his head and shrugged.

"Not looking like a big story. Retired librarian never got home from the airport." Lancaster leaned closer to Roha, and dropped his voice. "I think she probably had some kind of medical issue and wandered. Maybe got on another plane. Who knows? It's the best story I got going today."

Lancaster chuckled, and then glanced over his shoulder. "Some of her neighbors are about to go door-to-door with these flyers for her." He held up a missing person poster with Wanda Stroud's picture and details. "We're going to tag along with them. Want to join us?"

"No thanks." She smiled. "I'll just poke around here."

Lancaster took another lingering look at her. "Good meeting you, Sabrena."

Soledad nodded to her.

After they left, Roha went to other people at the tape, identified herself, and asked for Colleen Eden.

"We expect Colleen to join us at any moment," said a woman holding a small dog in her arms.

Roha thanked her, then stepped aside. She checked her phone for messages; more had come in. Some of her sources directed her to others; some promised to get back to her. And one person left a message saying only, "This could be an interesting one for you." Roha was going to call back when a shadow fell across her phone.

"Hello, I'm Colleen Eden. We're supposed to meet."

A woman in her 60s—blue eyes, high cheekbones, almost the same height as Roha—stood before her.

"Yes. Hello. Thank you." Roha shook her hand.

They stepped across the street, using the shade of a tree to talk in private. Looking at Wanda Stroud's house, Eden related her friend's life, the death of her husband, and her health issues. Eden recounted the day Stroud had returned, texting her from the airport with a coffee date for the next day.

"I asked her how things went in Mexico, and she said not so good."

"What do you think that means?" Roha asked.

"Likely because she didn't get the answers she wanted from the doctors there, all related to her anxiety and worries about getting sick."

Eden looked away, blinking back tears.

"This is all so, so wrong, and I'm so scared for her."

Roha nodded.

"The last thing Wanda texted to me really frightens me now."

"What was that?"

Eden got her phone, scrolled through her text messages to show her the message.

A weird thing happened on the plane.

Absorbing and processing it, Roha blinked, and then asked Eden, "Weird, like what? What does this mean?"

"I don't know."

Eden shook her head, tears rolling down her face.

CHAPTER 11

Los Angeles, California

At Los Angeles International Airport, a dozen people concentrated on their computer screens; some had three or four at their desks.

Suspended high on the wall beyond their workstations were several large flat screens showing live images. The screens occasionally divided into smaller boxes of activity inside and outside of the facility's nine terminals.

This was LAX's Airport Response Coordination Center, a 24/7 operation where analysts from several law enforcement agencies monitored the 3,500 security cameras posted throughout the complex. The analysts at the center also kept watch on social media and chased down intel for possible threats. Over the years, LAX had been a target for attacks, and had seen violent incidents.

Wanda Stroud's case was a priority out of concern for her safety. The fact that her last known location was LAX also underscored the potential that her disappearance could be linked to a threat to airport operations.

The TSA and FBI were checking the flight's passenger manifest, investigating to see who was onboard and where they sat in relation to Stroud. Agents were checking passport swipes and identifications, running names against watch lists and no-fly lists, looking into backgrounds.

Police had obtained warrants to work with Stroud's carrier to locate her phone, gain access to all her data, including anything she may have stored online. They were also looking into any activity on her credit and banking cards after her arrival at LAX.

Got her, Elena Cortez, an airport police analyst, said to herself.

She'd been tasked with tracking Wanda Stroud from the moment she stepped from Cielo Ahora Flight CA359 at Terminal B, the Tom Bradley International Terminal.

Working from photos of Stroud, Cortez began tracking her on recorded footage as she moved down through the terminal, and down the escalator to the Customs and Border Protection area, where she joined the line working to the desks and CPB agents.

Scrutinizing the footage, Cortez saw Stroud conversing with a man waiting in the line. He was wearing jeans, and a navy jacket over a white shirt. He had a black-wheeled carry-on and a computer bag over his shoulder. Cortez made notes, then went back to footage showing Stroud and other passengers exiting Flight CA359.

The man was among them.

Cortez resumed watching Stroud on the recorded video. She cleared Customs and continued through the terminal to the baggage claim area. Tracking Stroud from various cameras, Cortez saw her take her phone from her bag and begin texting.

At the carousel, Stroud checked her phone again. Then, as bags from the flight emerged, she reached for a large one with a bright floral pattern, appearing to struggle with it. A man stepped over to help. The same man from her flight she had talked with in the Customs line. He appeared to glance at her luggage ID tag. They talked, and then Stroud rolled her bag to the exit alone.

Using other camera angles, Cortez saw the man talking on his phone.

Switching to other cameras, Cortez picked up Stroud getting into a long line at the taxi area where she waited to be assigned a cab.

Cortez went back to track the man, angles changing as the cameras captured him going to a dark blue sedan in a zone nearby. The driver opened the trunk, placed the man's luggage there. Both men glanced in the same direction, as if watching something. The man got into the back seat. Cortez tracked the sedan, which moved a short distance before stopping in a tow-away zone. It was directly across from the taxi line, where Stroud was still waiting for a cab.

Cortez leaned closer to her screen as the cameras showed the man leave the back seat of the sedan and approach Stroud. They appeared to talk as he took her bag and gestured to the sedan, where the driver had opened the trunk. The driver hefted Stroud's flower-patterned bag into the trunk.

Stroud got into the back seat of the sedan with the man.

The driver got behind the wheel.

The sedan left.

Cortez typed commands on her keyboard, and a clear image of the sedan's California plate filled her screen.

Cortez picked up her phone and called her supervisor.

"Nick, it's Cortez. I think I've got something on our missing woman."

CHAPTER 12

Queens, New York City

True Signal's news Sked scrolled on Ray Wyatt's laptop.

A ping sounded, and a message popped up.

"Anything for me, Ray?" Agnes Finney, at the news desk, asked.

"Nothing today," he wrote back.

"Okay. Let us know if you want me to send you any leads?"

Send me leads?

Wyatt took a moment. He interpreted Agnes Finney's note as a subtle nudge, because he hadn't given her anything for the Sked for some time.

"No, that's fine," he wrote. "Got a few things I'm looking into."

"All right. Thanks," Agnes said.

Since breaking the Hydra case, Wyatt hadn't produced many stories of any weight. He wanted to get back in the mix, but none of his ideas had grabbed him. And now...now...

How can I even think of a story with McDade's revelation screaming in my brain?

He wished McDade had allowed him to copy the new picture of Danny. Seeing Danny at six, Danny now, his face, his eyes, *Lisa's eyes, Lisa's cheeks*…The image had seared itself onto his mind.

In all the time after the fire, there were moments—small, hellish moments—when Wyatt accepted Danny's death. But those moments were short-lived, especially after he lost Lisa. She never, ever, gave up believing, and told Wyatt with her dying words: *Find Danny, Ray. Bring him home.*

Now, after all these agonizing years, McDade had given him the promise, and a glimpse of what was real.

That Danny was alive—could be alive.

Soft clicking on the floor pulled Wyatt from his thoughts. Molly, Wyatt's black lab, came to him, and placed her head on his lap. He stroked her ears.

"I think your nails may be due for a trim," he said.

She nuzzled him.

"I know what you want, okay?"

Wyatt went to the pantry and got Molly a treat—a soft-baked beef biscuit.

Then he found himself standing in the doorway of Danny's room, looking at it—untouched from when their world had stopped.

Taking stock, a warm feeling rolled over him.

He remembered how Lisa had decorated it for Danny. "You're not a baby anymore, sweetie. You're a big boy."

There was Danny's bed, still made with a *Star Wars* comforter, a stuffed SpongeBob SquarePants leaning against the pillow. There was Danny's white desk, his storage baskets for his toys. Above, a tiny Cessna hung with fishing line from the ceiling. When turned on, it flew in circles, its lights blinking. Wyatt got the plane for him when he'd been on assignment in Houston.

Wyatt sat on the bed, loving Danny's art on the walls. Finger painting and crayon drawings. Stick people smiling, all sunshine and happiness.

He looked to the low bookshelf, with Danny's favorite picture books.

He turned to the night table, reaching for the moose figurine—Danny's beloved toy that he and Lisa had bought at a gift shop in Banff on their vacation. It was tiny, made of bronzed cast iron, and stood on a marble base. On its underside were the words: *Danny Wyatt, Banff Canada*. Wyatt had used a knife to scratch Danny's name there.

Danny loved his little moose.

Wyatt traced his fingers over it, recalling how, after the fire in Banff, weeks had turned into months, with no trace of Danny except his cherished moose toy. Canadian officials had sent it to them by FedEx with a letter of condolence.

It was blackened. One of the antlers had broken off.

He touched his fingers to the letters he'd carved into the base.

Danny's name had survived.

Wyatt dragged his hand over his face, unable to stop the memories from rocketing him back through time....

Searching for Danny...crawling on his stomach...deeper into the suffocating, disorienting smoke...calling him...his fingers finding Danny's hand...seeing his terrified face streaked with soot, his eyes bulging...then his hand holding only air as something jerked Danny from him, dragged him back into the churning black clouds of the inferno—

"Daddy!"

Jolted back to the present, Wyatt went to the bedroom window. Outside, he saw a child in a helmet wobbling on a two-wheeled bicycle, the father trotting alongside.

"Daddy, I'm doing it! I'm doing it!"

Wyatt smiled.

Then, he glanced at the moose in his hand.

What am I doing here? Danny's alive, and what am I doing?

Wyatt went to his laptop.

DeCastilla's warnings about interfering—about the risk of jeopardizing the FBI's investigation to find Danny and other children—echoed in Wyatt's head, but he pushed them aside.

Danny was alive when I had his hand in the fire, and I lost him.

McDade believes Danny's still alive.

I can't sit back and lose him a second time.

CHAPTER 13

The Bronx, New York City

Unique Connex Used Computers was near the south end of the Bronx Zoo, north of the Cross Bronx Expressway at the edge of the West Farms section of the borough.

Wyatt wanted to go somewhere out of Queens for this.

An electric chime sounded when he entered. The place had the kind of dark wood paneling you'd find in your grandfather's basement in Corona. Every shelf was crammed with laptops, desktops, monitors, and an array of components.

The man behind the counter peered over bifocals from his phone.

"Yes?"

"I'm looking for a used, newer model laptop."

"We got everything, from cheaper, small Dells up to Microsoft Pro 7s, to MacBook Pros. You want one for gaming, graphics, or the basics?"

"The basics. But powerful."

The man showed him several models before suggesting a high-powered notebook with a 16-inch screen.

"Like new. Fifteen hundred," he said, turning it on.

"I'll take it," Wyatt said. "I'll pay cash."

Wyatt knew the store had a security camera, but he wanted to do all he could to reduce his trail. Besides, he wasn't doing anything illegal. He needed a clean computer that he planned to use to access free wireless Internet service wherever a network was available.

"Cash?" the man said.

"Is that okay?"

Sticking out his bottom lip, the man nodded.

"Also," Wyatt said. "There's software, or an app, I need installed. I don't know much about computers, so can you help me set it up now?"

"Now?"

"Yes."

Counting the cash and putting it in the register, the man said, "What kind of software or app do you need?"

"A dark web browser."

"I see. And you want it now?"

"Yes."

"Wait."

Wyatt watched the man go to the back where a younger man was hunched over a table working on a disassembled laptop. The two talked, glancing at Wyatt, before the man returned.

"It'll cost you another two hundred," he said.

Wyatt counted it off, relieved he'd withdrawn more than enough from the bank.

The younger man took Wyatt's laptop, gestured to him to follow him to his table. After Wyatt explained what he needed, the man began working—typing commands, having Wyatt create and enter passwords. Wyatt wrote them in the small notepad he kept in his back pocket. It took some time before the younger man finished, turning the laptop to Wyatt, moving the cursor to the few icons on the screen.

"This one will get you to free Internet networks, wherever they are, so you won't need to pay a provider for an account. This one connects you online traditionally—Google, Bing, etc. This one is your dark web browser."

Wyatt nodded.

"Now, with this, your location is hidden. You can't be tracked. Your anonymity is nearly one hundred percent secure. Still, some people may see your browsing activity."

"Thanks," Wyatt said. The younger man shut things down, and Wyatt collected his laptop.

"Buddy," the man said, "not my business why you want to go there, but a word to the wise?"

"What's that?"

"Be careful."

***

The footage showed a man in his 20s on his knees in the desert, hands and ankles bound. Behind him a masked man with a large knife stood behind him speaking in Spanish.

"This is what happens to our enemies."

For the next minute, the video, its sound up, image clear, shows the bound man's beheading by a drug cartel executioner.

It was one of the many horrible, disturbing things Wyatt had found when he went to the dark side of the dark web in search of his son. Like Dante's journey through Hell, Wyatt saw humanity at its worst. He came upon tutorials on how to cook and eat humans; videos of torture; pedophilia; drug trafficking; illicit arms and weapons for sale. In many cases, the style of the web pages looked different, with the text often hard to read.

For days, with no word from DeCastilla, and nothing from McDade, Wyatt searched for his son. In every spare moment, he went to coffee shops, fast food outlets, or parks near storefronts, anyplace that had free Internet access. He always sat with his back to the wall so no one could see his screen, taking steps to ensure no one saw what he saw. He kept the sound low, and used headphones as he searched for Danny.

Through human smuggling, he sought information on international adoptions; he created a false identity. He suggested in sites and forums that he was looking to adopt a boy about six. Inevitably, it led him to dead ends, depraved responses, disgusting places, or worse.

The problem was, Wyatt didn't know what he was doing.

He reflected on the previous time he'd attempted searching for Danny on the dark web. It was not long after the Royal Canadian Mounted Police and Alberta's Chief Medical Examiner had sent the last of their letters, reports, and documents on the fire. Canadian officials could find no trace of Danny, so they concluded that he'd been consumed in the inferno. Danny's death, like the others, was ruled an accident, not a crime—which meant no further investigation into the hotel fire that had claimed so many lives.

But without proof, Wyatt and Lisa didn't believe their son was dead. That prompted Wyatt to step up his efforts to find Danny, including using the dark web. At that time, Wyatt was still working with the First Press Alliance wire service, and his efforts led him to nothing but hardcore porn sites and other revolting online activities.

His search was discovered by his editors. While understanding the reason, they ordered Wyatt to cease, fearing he could open the door to a virus that would infect the wire service's networks.

He backed off.

Now, with that disaster fresh in his memory, and the warning from the computer tech at the Bronx shop, Wyatt's frustration mounted.

Even with a newer computer and better software, it was still futile.

Wyatt shut down his laptop, pulled his headphones off, and rubbed his tired eyes.

The thought that Danny was alive but lost somewhere in the world of the dark web horrified him.

Wyatt couldn't do this alone. He needed help.

CHAPTER 14

Manhattan, New York City

Maybe today will bring us one step closer.
At her desk in the FBI's New York headquarters at 26 Federal Plaza in Lower Manhattan, Jill McDade examined the Hydra case.

The ritualistic, unsolved murders across several states were central, of course. Slowly, the task force was confirming how each one was committed by Lasius Byyle, known as the Hydra Killer.

But there were tentacles.

It was through that ongoing, painstaking investigative work in the aftermath of Byyle's death that an intense new challenge had surfaced, one indicating that children were in jeopardy.

They knew Byyle abducted and murdered people. It appeared he kept some of the women alive, posed them as if they were art, photographed them, then offered them for sale online. If he couldn't complete a sale, he would kill them.

While analyzing and assessing Byyle's electronic devices, the FBI's cyber experts had pursued his online activity into the most dangerous realms of the dark web. But many of the sites had vanished, likely due to the extensive media coverage of the Hydra's death, McDade reasoned.

Still, the FBI, using methods to hide the fact they were law enforcement, continued probing. They picked up fragments, doorways to other networks, that may have been related to Byyle's travels and activities, whether he was directly involved or not. That's how they discovered what appeared to be a marketplace used by an illegal international adoption network. But they had not yet confirmed if Byyle was a player in that network.

The instant the FBI accessed it, the criminals, suspecting infiltration, launched a virus attack against the intruders. Barely thwarting it, the FBI backed off, but not before capturing several screen shots of what looked like a catalog of children available for intercountry adoption.

It was clearly illicit because accompanying each entry was an order number and dollar figure.

The problem was that the FBI had not obtained any further intel on the criminals.

Nothing.

From her window on the 28th floor, McDade glanced at the Brooklyn Bridge.

They could be anywhere in the world.

A soft knock sounded at her doorway.

"They're ready, Jill," Ed Sanders, one of the agents on the case, said.

"Thanks. Be right there."

Closing her files, she collected her tablet, notebook, and phone, and started down the hall, thinking how they had nothing but a glimpse of photos and concerns over the children.

Who are they? Where did they come from?

McDade, with others on the task force, had worked with age progression and facial recognition experts to check the faces from the screen shots against unsolved cases of missing children across the U.S. They sent alerts to every FBI office in the U.S., to every FBI legal attaché located in U.S. embassies, and to every police database in the country. They submitted photos to

Interpol, and consulted national and international missing children's groups.

For good measure, McDade submitted photos of Danny Wyatt.

So far, three older cases came back—that of a four-year-old girl, missing from Toronto, Canada, and then a three-year-old boy, who had disappeared in Spain. Both cases, while cold, were under active investigation by police in those countries, who were also working with McDade and the Hydra task force to find the people behind the adoption ring.

Then, McDade was stunned when she was alerted to the third case, with a near-perfect age-progressed match.

Danny Wyatt.

After anguishing over the decision, McDade told Wyatt about Danny, without informing anyone else that she had. In her heart, she believed Wyatt deserved to know. She also wanted an extra layer of identification for the investigation.

She trusted him to keep her confidence and not get involved.

At least long enough for us to investigate, locate these people, and make arrests.

She came to the meeting room, standing outside for a moment.

Right now, I don't know how long that will be, because we have nothing. We need all the help we can get, and this morning we're taking a long shot.

She opened the door.

***

At the table, Devlin Foxe, the only known associate of Lasius Byyle, was flanked by Grady Newland, his attorney, and Robert Mills, another lawyer from an affiliated New York firm.

Across from them were Ed Sanders and two other agents.

After the introductions, Newland looked at McDade. "Agent McDade, this session could've been done virtually, instead of insisting we drive down here from Vermont."

"We prefer this be done face-to-face," McDade said.

"As you know," Newland said, "my client is awaiting sentencing, and had to request the court adjust his bail conditions to come here."

"Yes."

"The court allowed us this consideration to further demonstrate his desire to cooperate."

"We're aware and supported the bail adjustment," McDade said.

"Then you, being a leading agent on this case, are aware my client has already cooperated fully, told you what he could concerning the late Mr. Byyle."

"New information has surfaced."

"What new information?" Newland said.

McDade related a summary of how the FBI obtained the screen shots of the children offered on the dark web, and that Byyle's online activity led them there. She then cued up the screen shots of the children on her tablet, and turned it to Foxe and Newland.

They saw the gallery of head-and-shoulder pictures of young faces, each with a catalog number and a dollar figure in U.S. currency, some upward of $250,000.

Foxe traded a look with Newland.

"We want Mr. Foxe to tell us everything he knows about this activity," McDade said.

Foxe remained silent.

"Mr. Foxe, you've been charged with a long list of offences—fraud, tax fraud, aiding and abetting Mr. Byyle. Your sentencing is still an open question, your cooperation being a key factor. We've established the fact that we consider you Mr. Byyle's associate—"

"Now, hold on. He was never an associate," Newland said.

"If I may continue, Mr. Newland," McDade said. "You associated with Mr. Byyle, and we still have your devices as evidence in the case. Are you prepared to tell us right now all you know about this specific activity relating to these children, and any other activity?"

Foxe looked to Newland for help.

"Agent McDade, may my client and I have a moment alone?"

McDade nodded. Then she and the agents left the room.

***

Less than five minutes later, Newland opened the door.

McDade and the agents returned.

"My client wishes to continue to cooperate fully," Newland said.

Foxe's knuckles whitened as he clasped his hands on the table.

"Look, I had nothing to do with that adoption thing," he began.

Foxe related what the agents knew—that he had a fetish; that he liked to watch other people doing weird, kinky things to each other live online. Foxe said he satisfied his desires on the dark web, which is where he met Byyle. It led to Foxe illegally—and lucratively—renting an estate property to Byyle in a remote corner of Vermont, where he lived off the grid.

"I had no idea who he was," Foxe said. "I admit to meeting him on the dark web, where I satisfied my desires. I had no idea what he was up to. He guarded his privacy."

"But in your travels, you had some knowledge of this adoption network, correct?"

"Yes. I was aware of chatter and discussion of this adoption activity on the dark web," Foxe said. "But I had no interest in it, and had no idea Byyle was involved."

"What kind of chatter?" McDade said.

Foxe swallowed.

"That it operated outside of the U.S."

"Where?"

Foxe shook his head.

"Some rumors were that it was an enterprise run by extremely dangerous people."

"Do you have any idea where the operation's located?"

"I don't know, but I remember that someone said it was a different kind of adoption network."

"Different how?"

"People shopped for what legitimate adoption agencies couldn't offer."

"I don't understand."

"The children were 'replacement' children."

"Replacement?" McDade repeated.

"Wealthy people from around the world, grieving over losing a child, would be willing to pay huge amounts to illegally adopt one that looked the same—you know, gender, age, resemblance—to replace their dead child."

CHAPTER 15

Los Angeles, California

Navigating through San Pedro, Mateo Lopez parked his mother's Nissan at the specific location down around South Seaside, turned to his friend, Noah Miller, and smiled.

"This is it. All set?" Mateo said.

"Ready."

Anticipation growing, they got out, checking to make sure no one else was watching. It looked good. Then, using his phone, Noah began recording as—according to detailed directions they'd found online—they walked to the opening in the first chain-link fence. Slipping through it, they came to the second fence, and another opening.

They passed through it.

"We're in," Noah said, continuing to record, panning the complex of abandoned warehouses at the Port of Los Angeles.

Mateo and Noah were urban explorers—people who commonly write, photograph, and post about their visits to abandoned sites and buildings. They knew it was illegal, because it was clearly trespassing, and risky, because of the dangers of aged, neglected structures. But the activity was growing in popularity around the world, and most urban explorers were respectful.

Mateo and Noah had already been to many sites in California.

The old warehouse complex at the port was on their list.

Moving across pavement—blistered, potholed, with weeds rising through cracks—they neared the cluster of half a dozen buildings.

Some stood two stories high; others had nearly six levels. Their massive doorways opened to vast empty areas nearly as large as a football field. The steel beams of the support frames were rusted, tired. Corrugated walls displayed colorful graffiti. Windows were filthy or missing glass.

An eerie silence filled the air.

With Noah still recording, broken glass, nails, bolts, and bits of crumbled cement crunched underfoot as they continued. They were glad they always wore their heavy steel-toed boots to protect them while exploring.

Passing to other buildings, they saw old signs designating equipment areas, others cautioning about safety. They came to massive heavy machinery, sitting idle, laced with dirt, and rusting.

In one multilevel building, they climbed stairs, checking out level after level. They entered a corner room—an office, with a rotting wooden desk, its drawers open, letters and documents left behind.

"Hey, remember the legend?" Noah said.

Mateo nodded.

In some circles, explorers in New York, or Chicago, or maybe it was Philadelphia, found a metal box with thousands of dollars in cash. Many suspected it had been hidden and forgotten after a bank robbery.

Most considered it an urban myth.

Mateo and Noah moved to another building, which held a system of pipes and controls, along with square pits in the floor. Moving through it, they came to a labyrinth of rooms, most with closed doors.

One was marked DANGER HIGH VOLTAGE KEEP OUT.

They obeyed.

In another, they found a workbench with rusted tools on it.

Moving along, they came to a door half-opened to darkness.

Mateo and Noah exchanged glances, then nodded. Noah was recording.

Mateo pulled out his flashlight, while slowly pushing the door open wider. They were hit with a wall of foul, putrid air.

The door protested with a creepy creaking as Mateo illuminated the dark room. The walls dripped with water leaking from the floor above. Below, carved into the floor was a large, deep, rectangular pit.

Mateo, covering his mouth and nose with one hand— Noah did the same while recording—stepped closer to the edge of the pit.

It reached down about 10 feet, to dark water.

Mateo's light caught movement of something furry with a tail splashing.

"Rats," Mateo said.

"What the f—!" Noah shouted.

They spotted a human hand, foot, and part of a skull just breaking the water's surface, quivering where more rats were feasting.

CHAPTER 16

Los Angeles, California

The woman in dark glasses lifted her head from her phone to watch Sabrena Roha approaching her bench.

They had agreed to meet in MacArthur Park.

In the time since Roha went to Downey—where she'd learned that the last thing Wanda Stroud texted before she vanished was that a weird thing had happened on the plane from Mexico—Roha had continued digging into the story.

What weird thing? It was cryptic, a mystery.

Roha pushed her sources, including Maria Quiroz, the woman waiting for her on the park bench.

A few years back, Roha had reported on working conditions for Mexico's flight attendants. Quiroz, an official with one of Mexico's flight attendants' unions, had become a good source. Roha had reached out to her for help on the missing woman, giving her the usual assurances of anonymity.

Quiroz, who was in Los Angeles on business, had agreed to do what she could for Roha, suggesting they meet in the park, which was not far from the Mexican Consulate.

After greeting each other with hugs and small talk, they got on with things, speaking in Spanish.

"I located the attendants who were on Cielo Ahora Flight CA359," Quiroz said. "And you're right. Something serious is going on concerning that flight."

"What can you tell me?"

"Mexican federal police and police in Mexico City are working with their U.S. counterparts, the FBI, and others."

"Doing what, exactly?"

"Well, as you indicated, the focus is on the missing California woman."

"Wanda Stroud, yes."

"They've been asking questions about her and the flight."

"What sort of questions?"

Quiroz held up a finger, then went to her phone—tapping commands, making a call, waiting as it rang.

"I've been talking to the attendants, and I've got one willing to talk to you—but she's nervous." Quiroz kept her finger up, and then began speaking into her phone. A moment later, she continued in Spanish, reassuring the person on the line before passing her phone to Roha.

"Hi," the woman on the line said. "Maria said it's safe to talk to you. You won't use my name."

"Of course. I don't know your true name. But for our conversation, what can I call you?"

"Brisa."

"Thank you, Brisa. I won't use Brisa. I'll protect you by referring to the information as coming from an unnamed source, which could be anyone—law enforcement, LAX people, anyone. Okay?"

"I think so. All right."

"So, you were an attendant on the flight?"

"Yes."

"What did police ask you?"

"They were very interested in the demeanor and actions of the missing woman in 15B."

"Like what?"

"If she seemed frightened or alarmed, or if there were any issues with the passengers around her."

"Were there?"

"Not really. She asked for water, but nothing really. She had her row to herself, and there was no one near, except for the man ahead of her at the window in 14A."

"Were there issues with him?"

"No. He seemed like a serious business type, working on his laptop. But he lowered the screen a little each time we passed."

"And that's it? Did the police indicate anything?"

"Well, they asked if I thought the woman might have seen something on the man's laptop from her seat that might've upset her."

"Really? Like what? Porn? Something like that?"

"They didn't say. But I told them at one point, we thought we saw the woman taking photos in the cabin during the flight."

"Photos of what?"

"We're not sure, but police asked us if we thought she was taking photos of his computer. We said it was possible, but we weren't sure."

"Did you see anything on his computer?"

"No."

Roha thought, then said, "Do you have this man's name? Was he American? Mexican?"

"No, I don't know."

"Could you get me his name from the manifest?"

Brisa let a long moment pass before saying, "Let me speak to Maria."

Quiroz and the woman spoke for several minutes, and then Quiroz ended the call.

"She's scared, Sabrena. Police were strict about not revealing any part of their investigation."

Roha understood.

"But we trust you, and a woman is missing," Quiroz said. "I'll work with her and our people to get the man's name without arousing police suspicion."

Roha took hold of Quiroz's knee, squeezing it.

"Thank you, Maria, and please thank Brisa. This means a lot to me."

They hugged, ending their meeting.

As she walked from the park to her Mustang, Roha's phone rang with a blocked number. Many of her sources blocked their numbers.

"Roha," she answered.

"Hey, it's Madison."

Roha recognized her friend, the forensic analyst who was working at Wanda Stroud's house in Downey.

"Hey right back."

"Listen, you didn't get this from me, okay?"

"Sure." Roha surveyed the area around her to ensure she had some privacy. "What is it?"

"They found something in San Pedro you might want to check out, and now the FBI is bigfooting the case."

"What is it?"

"Gotta go."

CHAPTER 17

Manhattan, New York

The next morning, Ray Wyatt joined the nearly 2,000 people boarding the Staten Island Ferry at the Whitehall Ferry Terminal in Lower Manhattan.

Taking the stairs to an upper deck, he scanned the area near a food concession, and spotted a man wearing a Mets cap and a white T-shirt with a sugar skull on it.

The man, who had a backpack at his feet, was sitting alone, looking out the window, when Wyatt took a seat next to him.

"You found me," the man said.

Wyatt set his newly acquired laptop on the bench between them, and said, "Thanks for helping me, Bill."

"I haven't done anything, yet," the man said, giving Wyatt a smile.

"Meeting me is a start. Thanks."

"No problem."

"Like I said, we need to keep this confidential."

"Absolutely."

Bill Garvin was Wyatt's colleague before the deepest round of staff cuts at First Press Alliance, the worldwide wire service where Garvin headed IT support. After the layoffs, Garvin landed a position with a cybersecurity company. Wyatt had always considered him an expert.

Like everyone at the First Press Alliance, Garvin, who'd known Wyatt for years, was sympathetic to his tragedy. So, when Wyatt called Garvin yesterday seeking his help searching for Danny on the dark web, he agreed.

"But like I told you on the phone, Ray, I'm not optimistic," Garvin said, pulling his laptop from his backpack as the ferry left the dock for Staten Island.

"I appreciate any help." Wyatt turned on his computer.

Free WiFi was available at the terminal and on the boat.

"Log on to your computer. I'll first install antivirus programs for you."

Wyatt logged on. Then Garvin went online and installed the programs, which took some time.

"All right," Garvin said. "Now, after you outlined everything on our call, I found a couple of pretty good apps to help us—one for facial recognition, and one for age enhancement. I'll load them onto your unit."

When the security programs finished, Garvin began loading the apps.

"Give me the best photo you have of Danny's face."

Wyatt provided Garvin a photo, and Garvin began processing it, in an attempt to replicate the photo McDade had shown Wyatt.

"Ray, the FBI's technology will far exceed that of the apps I just loaded. Also, the stuff that's available to us works better on photos of people in the 15-to-60 age range; this isn't a precise science, so keep that in mind."

Using the apps, it took Garvin several minutes to produce a photo of Danny at age six.

"Pretty good," Wyatt said. "It looks similar to what McDade showed me."

"Okay. Now, I'm going to equip your system with a program I created to run our age-progressed image through the dark web, to see if we can find the source of Danny's photo that the FBI found."

"Let's do it," Wyatt said.

"Remember, because the dark web is not the same as the conventional web most of the world uses, its characteristics are different, which means this might not work at all."

Garvin launched his program, using the age-enhanced photo they just created to search the dark web for Danny.

An icon was flashing on a blank blue screen, showing that it was searching. A solid minute went by without a result, then another minute.

Then a new page appeared, like a lightning flash, showing a gallery of children's faces, before it vanished. It all happened in under a second.

"What the —?" Garvin said.

The blinking icon froze.

Suddenly, the fan on Wyatt's laptop whirred loudly, as if the hard drive was overworked. New toolbars appeared. Garvin tried closing them, but his commands were ignored.

A series of death's-head pop-up windows began blossoming on the screen.

"We're being attacked," Garvin said.

Any command Garvin initiated was ignored.

"What?"

Garvin flipped over the laptop and removed the battery, shutting it down. Then he shook his head.

"I think we knocked on their door, Ray, but—"

"But what?"

"We're not getting in."

"Can we try again?"

Garvin shook his head.

"These guys are good, Ray. They may have just fried your laptop. I'll take it home and see if I can fix it for you."

"I don't care. I'll get another computer. We have to keep trying."

"Ray, I'm sorry. I never thought this through. This is dangerous."

"Danny's out there. That's what's more dangerous."

"I know. I'm sorry, but whoever's behind this has some heavy-duty skill. I've never encountered something so immediately aggressive."

"We can't stop. We're talking about my son."

"I know, Ray. But there are so many risks. If the FBI caught us, we could be charged for interfering with an investigation."

Wyatt shook his head and turned away.

"Ray, let me work on your laptop, and think about what we can do."

Wyatt nodded as the boat's big diesel engines slowed, and it eased into the St. George Ferry Terminal on Staten Island.

After docking, Wyatt thanked Garvin, who had business on Staten Island, and left.

Wyatt joined the crowd for the next ferry back to Manhattan.

During his return trip, dejected in his defeat, he looked at the Statue of Liberty when his phone rang.

"Ray, it's DeCastilla. Got a sec?"

"Hey, Tony. Sure."

"Listen, I just want you to know that I haven't forgotten. I'm working on things. Just hang in there."

CHAPTER 18

Los Angeles, California

As Wanda Stroud smiled from the screen, Special Agent Cal Banner took stock of her face at his desk in the FBI's Los Angeles office on Wilshire.

She could be anyone's mother, or grandmother.

Years ago, while in college, Stroud had worked part-time in the Downey police records department. Her employee fingerprints were still on file, and the Los Angeles County Medical Examiner-Coroner's office used them to identify her as the homicide victim discovered in an abandoned warehouse at the Port of Los Angeles in San Pedro.

Preliminary findings indicated she was shot at close range in the back of the head, evocative of an execution-style murder.

Why kill a 66-year-old widowed librarian from Downey?

Stroud's murder, after she'd vanished from LAX upon her arrival in the U.S. from a trip to Mexico City, was a priority, and Banner had been assigned to it from the get-go. Now that it was a homicide with international aspects, Banner's boss, Supervisory Special Agent Robin Dixon, advised him that the FBI would lead the multiagency investigation, which included Mexican law enforcement and Interpol.

"And you're the case agent, Cal," Dixon said.

Banner channeled the pressure.

He always did—refining it to an all-consuming, laser focus on the work, to the exclusion of everything else in his life, according to his ex-wife.

Eighteen months after his divorce, Banner had transferred from the FBI's Chicago office to L.A. and threw himself into the job. He worked nonstop on cases, including the investigation that led to the arrests of several gang members who'd committed a string of armed robberies and shootings in Beverly Hills.

Now, after a year and a half in Los Angeles, Banner was still using unpacked boxes for furniture in his barely affordable apartment in Westwood. Last night, he'd stood at stacked boxes filled with books, eating tacos while examining every statement, report, image, and lead on Stroud, again and again.

She saw something. Something happened on that plane.

This morning, at his desk in the office, Banner finished his coffee, collected his tablet, phone, notebook, and files. He went to the large boardroom to head the first case-status meeting in the wake of Stroud's death.

Investigators from Downey, LAX, LAPD, L.A. County, state, and federal agencies settled in around the table. On the line were detectives with Mexican law enforcement and the FBI's legal attaché in Mexico City.

Dixon did a quick roll call of introductions. Banner made a wireless connection with his tablet to the wall monitor at one end of the room, and then got rolling.

"We've got a lot to cover. You have the updated summaries," Banner began. "Since this case emerged, a lot of good work was started. We're building on it."

The wall monitor came to life with photos of Stroud, while Banner related known details of her homicide.

The monitor then showed the face of a man in his 50s—white hair, good-looking, serious expression—on a passport photo. His name: José Luís Garcia.

"We believe he is an attorney based in Honduras," Banner said. "Garcia is the man who was seated in the row ahead of Stroud."

Banner went through a montage of security camera clips and stills, tracking Stroud and Garcia through LAX to the taxi pickup zone, ending with her getting into a dark blue sedan with Garcia and his driver.

"Garcia is our key person of interest," Banner said. "We've dug into his background, and the intel emerging via Interpol from police around the world is troubling."

A slide on the monitor showed Garcia—also known as Alberto Aiza, Felix Neri, and Victor Nyllev—as having a number of professional occupations, more than a dozen aliases, and passports from several countries, including Canada, Mexico, and the U.S, where he had 10 Social Security numbers.

Brenner noted that Garcia was suspected of having worked for global money launderers in Panama, Russia, and the Caribbean, for a counterfeiting network in Europe, and for drug cartels in Mexico, Central America, and South America.

"He's a powerful operator for some dangerous and extremely sophisticated organizations," Banner said.

"But he's always been an under-the-radar figure. Almost invisible, until now. Here's what we know. He boarded Cielo Ahora Flight CA359 in Mexico City to Los Angeles, occupied window seat 14A. Stroud was behind him in the middle seat, 15B. They each had rows to themselves, with no other passengers near."

Banner related how the flight attendants suggested Garcia was engrossed in his work, eyeing them, subtly lowering his screen whenever they walked by. Some attendants believed Stroud was photographing his screen, and that he became uneasy and snapped it shut. As for Stroud, one attendant thought she may have exhibited a trace of unease, but not unlike that of any nervous flyer.

"What about Stroud's movements in Mexico?" Trish Morgan, an LAPD detective, asked.

"She went there for medical reasons, and it checks out, so far," Banner said.

"What about Garcia's movements?" Morgan asked.

"We know he boarded the flight," Miguel Fuentes, a Mexican investigator on the line, said. "We're endeavoring to track him prior. He may have used other identification to enter Mexico."

"What about the car used at LAX?" Kevin Sandoval, the FBI's legal attaché, asked over the line.

"We got the plate," Banner said. "The vehicle was rented in L.A. through a numbered company, which led to a labyrinth of numbered companies and stolen credit cards. We've yet to locate the car or identify the driver."

"What about activity on Stroud's credit and bank cards?" Larry Cox, an agent with Homeland, asked.

"Subsequent to her return, none," Banner said.

"Where are we with Stroud's phone?" Morgan said. "Her phone is critical."

Before Banner could answer, Sandoval, in Mexico, said, "Maybe a cartel's using her as an unwitting mule, and something went wrong? What do we think happened?"

Banner glanced at his boss, and Dixon nodded for him to go ahead.

"We can speculate while adhering to the known facts," Banner said. "Stroud was seated behind Garcia, who had his laptop open. Stroud texted her friend about a 'weird' happening on the plane, and Garcia left LAX with Stroud. We believe Stroud saw something on Garcia's laptop."

"Like what?" Sandoval asked.

"We don't know at this stage," Banner said.

"Having her phone would help," Morgan said.

"Detective Chambers in Downey started the process to obtain Stroud's phone records and data," Banner said. "We followed that with a warrant. We're working with

Stroud's provider on unlocking her stored data. We've not located her phone so far. The last signal was from the LAX area. Then it went silent."

"Was this around the time she departed with Garcia?" Sandoval asked.

"Yes," Banner said. "Her provider says she may have been using an online digital storage service for her data. We're attempting to access that."

"So, we don't know what she saw, if she saw anything?" Morgan said.

"That may be the case," Banner said. "But I believe Stroud saw something on Garcia's computer, and whatever it was, it cost her her life."

CHAPTER 19

Los Angeles, California

The meeting wrapped up.

Investigators left the room, while Banner and Dixon stayed behind discussing next steps.

"Cal, let's try obtaining security camera footage from the company where Garcia's people leased the car."

"We did, but the company's archive has malfunctioned."

"Then we go to the host company for another shot at the footage," Dixon said. She turned, hearing a soft knock at the open doorway. "Yes, Olivia?"

"Excuse me." Special Agent Olivia Hinson had left the meeting but returned, glancing at her phone. "I just heard back from our cyber people, and they've sent us something we need to see."

Banner went to his tablet as a secure email with attachments arrived.

"Got it," he said.

"It's what they found in Stroud's digital data storage," Hinson said. "The timing aligns, indicating that either Stroud stored it, or it was stored automatically when she arrived at LAX."

"Shut the door, please, Olivia," Dixon said. "Cal, put it up on the big monitor."

Banner entered a few commands on his tablet, and the large screen on the wall displayed the first in a series of still photos Stroud had taken on the plane.

They showed the man in the row in front of her, working on his computer with a screen large enough for her to see what was on it.

"That's got to be Garcia," Hinson said.

The series of photos zoomed in on the images on the man's screen.

Faces of children, uniformly framed, each labeled with a number, like a catalog.

Dixon began tapping her pen on the table as more photos displayed captured messages and snippets of sentences: *adoptee…agreement…transfer of rights to adoptive parents…will obtain a decree…facilitator…fees…will secure authentic-looking records and legal documents…validating legal status as an orphan…*

The next set of photos showed more communication: *Correct. This week, we have solid offers for #0247 from Madrid, #6796 from Melbourne, #0055 from Johannesburg, #2095 from Moscow, #8849 from Buenos Aires, #3716 from London and #9902 from Toronto. Then: Updating price list offerings now.*

After the last still photo was displayed, Banner clicked on the short video taken of the same subject and angle. They saw the same images and text, this time capturing faces, catalog numbers, and dollar figures in U.S. currency. Young faces and numbers flowed by: $185,000… $130,000…$155,000…

The man's typing stopped. He turned his head slightly before closing his laptop.

The video ended.

"Wow," Hinson said.

"This connects a lot of dots," Banner said. "Looks like he's running illegal adoptions."

Dixon's pen-tapping on the table stopped.

"This is what we do," she said. "We run these faces through our missing-person files, check against any alerts from other offices. We also run them through every database, everything. We reach out far and fast, to see if there's a connection to any other ongoing investigations, and we dig deeper on Garcia, working with Mexican authorities and Interpol."

Later, working alone at his desk, Banner looked at Stroud's photo.

Then he replayed the video. His jaw muscles pulsed as he stared at what he could see of Garcia, working away at selling children and murdering widows.

We're coming for you. Little by little, step by step. We're coming.

CHAPTER 20

Manhattan, New York City

Replacement children.

The revelation gnawed at Jill McDade.

What Devlin Foxe had told them about the network on the dark web was a break, but so far, her team had been unable to advance it.

After an intense day of following up on the alerts they'd put out to all bureaus, after checking with the FBI's cyber people, and chasing down investigative threads with little success, McDade headed home.

Replacement children. My God, she thought, glancing at toddlers with their parents as her subway train rumbled north to her stop at 157th Street and Broadway in Washington Heights.

McDade got a couple of take-out chicken dinners at the corner deli. Then she went to her building and the apartment of her friend, Gwen Lansing, who lived alone upstairs and watched Alison for her.

"Thanks again, Gwen. Sorry I'm a little late. I'll get her home and feed her." McDade waited at the door for Alison.

"Another challenging case, Jill?"

"Yup."

"I see it in your eyes." Gwen, a retired paramedic, touched McDade's shoulder. "Remember to breathe, sweetie."

In that moment, McDade reflected on all they'd been through, how Gwen had once said, "When life knocks you down, you get back up and knock it right back." That's what they did. They had endured together because Gwen was more than a friend—she was McDade's rock.

Alison appeared with her backpack. "All set, Mom."

"Look at her." Gwen smiled. "Just turned eleven, and already a young lady."

"Gwen, can we do some needlepoint next time?" Alison asked.

"Certainly." Then Gwen whispered into McDade's ear as they left: "Breathe."

Now with dinner done, and the mess cleaned up, McDade had surrendered her desk to Alison, who was doing homework, while she—with her tablet, phone, files, and notes spread on the kitchen table—resumed working.

She studied the other cases that age-enhancement and facial-recognition technology had tied to the adoption ring. There was the four-year-old boy missing from London, and the three-year-old girl, who'd vanished in Madrid. Both cases were cold, but McDade searched for more common denominators—anything else similar to the case of Danny Wyatt.

The British boy disappeared while with his family in London, near the Eye observation wheel; the Spanish girl, while with her father on the Madrid Metro. Beyond disappearing in a public place while with a parent, and being recorded in the catalog of an illicit adoption scheme, McDade failed to find more common links. No suspects or solid evidence had emerged in the disappearances.

Who's behind this operation?

Again, she looked at the screen shots of the children of the adoption ring they'd found through Byyle's activity on the dark web. She studied the gallery of young faces, with their catalog numbers and price tags.

Danny Wyatt's face was among them.

It pierced her.

She thought of Ray Wyatt and his anguish, how he had the right to know that Danny did not die in the hotel fire in Banff, Canada. After he'd told her of his hope of one day finding him, she felt she had to help him. She considered Ray's tragedies—losing Danny, then his wife—and then considered her own—losing Tim, her husband, to cancer, and then the terrible events with Alison. How could she not feel a bond with Ray?

It broke her heart thinking of him, haunted and living alone with his dog, Molly, in that house in Queens. Alison loved their visits. And while Alison still had sessions with her therapist, Doctor Orlov, Alison's bad dreams weren't as frequent as they used to be.

And she couldn't forget Gwen, solid and strong after all that had happened.

As for me? McDade released a weak, soft chuckle. *Who knows?*

She resumed working, asking the same questions.

Who is running the network, and where are the children?

She glanced out her window at the lights on the cables of the George Washington Bridge, linking New Jersey and New York City over the Hudson. They were pretty, and with a holiday weekend coming, the towers would be fully illuminated in a spectacular display.

McDade's phone vibrated and rang at the same time. She answered.

"Jill, it's Loren. Can you talk?"

She recognized the voice of her supervisor, Steve Loren.

"Yes."

"We've got a lead. Our L.A. office responded to our alert, matching our photos to photos in an active case there."

McDade sat straighter.

"Is it a good lead?"

"It's significant, involving a homicide."

"A homicide?"

"And international connections. Jill, this case just got a whole lot bigger. Our team is going to work with theirs. I'm going to connect you with the case agent in L. A., Special Agent Cal Banner. We'll want you to pursue this in California."

McDade looked up from her note-taking, and saw Alison staring at her as she ended her call.

"You look so serious, Mom. Is everything okay?"

McDade looked at her. But her thoughts were elsewhere before they returned to her daughter, who repeated her question.

"Yes, honey. Everything's okay. Is your homework done?"

CHAPTER 21

Alhambra, California

Sabrena Roha paused to read parts of what she'd written so far on Wanda Stroud's murder.

> *Stroud, a 66-year-old widowed librarian from Downey, California, vanished mysteriously after landing in Los Angeles on a return flight from Mexico City.*
>
> *"I can't comprehend why anyone would hurt her. Wanda was the kindest, gentlest soul," Colleen Eden, Stroud's friend, said through tears. "Who would do this?"*

Roha stopped reading, and reflected on her tip—how she'd driven to the scene in San Pedro. She'd managed to talk to the boys who found Stroud, and picked up a little color. Other than that, there wasn't much there.

She continued reading.

> *Stroud's body was discovered in a rat-infested pit in an abandoned warehouse at the Port of Los Angeles in San Pedro*

by two young men, self-described urban explorers.

A horrible place to die, Roha thought, turning to photos of Stroud, taking in her warm, friendly smile.

The kindest, gentlest soul.

Something inside tore at Roha every time she did a story like this. She felt for Colleen Eden and the people who loved Stroud because she knew the pain of losing someone. But she had to maintain a professional distance. She steeled herself. She had a job to do. Picking up her phone, she checked for new messages from her sources before returning to her notes and the story.

Investigators at the San Pedro scene were tight-lipped, which Roha had expected. She got the sense that the FBI was now leading, but no one at the scene would tell her. She'd made little progress there, because she didn't know any of the investigators. Later, the LAPD and Downey Police put out near identical bare-bones news releases, stating what was already known and nothing more.

But there was more to this case, much more.

A weird thing happened on the plane.

Flipping through her notes, Roha recalled the questions investigators had asked the flight attendants about the mysterious man on Stroud's plane seated in the row ahead of her. Biting her bottom lip, Roha searched for other recent reports on Stroud's homicide, in the *Los Angeles Times*, and on L.A.'s major TV news outlets. All were reporting the basics. If they knew more, they weren't reporting it.

Coming back to her story, Roha weighed how much information she should include at this stage.

Should I tip my hand now, when I know there's more to this story?

Her phone rang.

It was Maria Quiroz with the flight attendants' union.

"I have something new for you," Quiroz said in Spanish.

Roha picked up her pen, poised to take notes.

"Go ahead."

"Not on the phone."

"Where then?"

"I'm in Santa Monica at the amusement park with a friend's family. I'll get away for a moment, so meet me in one hour on the pier, the end of the longer one."

***

An hour later, Roha looked out at the Pacific, breathing in the air, watching the gulls gliding and screeching, the wind lifting her hair.

Below, waves rolled into the posts of the pier, crashing, sweeping, and rolling out again.

Roha felt a tap on her shoulder. Quiroz stood next to her, and they began.

"I don't have much time," Quiroz said.

"What do you know?"

"I spoke with a Cielo Ahora attendant who was not on the flight."

Quiroz glanced around to ensure they had privacy and lowered her voice.

"But the attendant's brother is a detective in Mexico City, and she had dinner with him last night. She's close to her brother. He's protective. So she told him she'd heard a rumor concerning an L.A.-bound passenger with her airline. He was having a few beers, and said he knew about it."

"What did he say?"

"He said he's part of the Stroud investigation, and is working with investigators here in California. The case is very serious. They think it's tied to a global network of illegal adoptions of children. I got the name of the man seated in front of the woman."

Quiroz passed Roha a folded piece of paper.

Roha opened it: José Luís Garcia, attorney, Honduras.

"Wow." Roha hugged Quiroz. "Thank you, Maria."

After their embrace, Quiroz clasped Roha's shoulders.

"Listen, Sabrena. Be careful. A woman has already been murdered."

"Yes, I know."

"The brother said they think this man, Garcia, is very dangerous, because he works for very dangerous people."

***

At her apartment, Roha finished typing up her notes from her meeting with Quiroz, and sat back, staring at her laptop screen and thinking.

She recalled her interview with Chase Lockner, managing editor of True Signal, and how he'd emphasized that the news agency's mission was to go beneath the surface, to get to the truth, and to break meaningful exclusives, no matter how long it took, or where it led.

Roha decided not to file a story.

Not yet.

She was just scratching the surface of this one. But it was time to let Anges Finney on the desk in New York know. Roha logged into the Sked and made her first entry of her story, with a slug, byline and short notes:

MURDERADOPTION, by Sabrena Roha, LOS ANGELES: The murder of a retired California librarian upon her return from Mexico may be linked to an illegal global adoption network. (Developing; may require travel.)

CHAPTER 22

Manhattan, New York

The High Line park rises on an abandoned rail line 30 feet over the streets below, zigzagging for more than a mile through Manhattan's west side.

Wyatt met DeCastilla at the Gansevoort Street and 23rd Street entrance, where they began walking and talking.

They hadn't gone far before DeCastilla told Wyatt that he'd obtained intel from a friend on the Hydra task force.

"There's a hot new lead tied to the illegal adoption ring."

"A hot new lead?" Wyatt looked at DeCastilla as he continued.

"What I got, Ray, is that it's connected to an ongoing investigation in Los Angeles, and the homicide of a woman who'd just returned from Mexico."

Wyatt stopped walking.

So did DeCastilla.

People flowed around them.

"A woman's murder? Did they find Danny? What else can you tell me, Tony?"

"That's it. What I get is that this is just happening, and that the California investigation is huge, and being led by the FBI."

They resumed walking, Wyatt's pulse quickening as they contemplated theories and scenarios while taking in the vistas. Amid the calm of the shrubs and trees, the crosstown views, and the sweep of the Hudson, Wyatt grappled with new waves of anguish for Danny as they ended their meeting.

"Keep the faith, Ray," DeCastilla said. "I'll keep working on this."

Wyatt thanked him, and then left for the long subway ride back to Queens.

The train rumbled and clattered as pillars and walls blurred by. Wyatt's thoughts swirled. The roll and sway of the subway pulled him back, back to the hotel fire….

I crawled…deeper into the smoke…feeling my way in the blistering heat…blind until my fingers found Danny's hand….I could feel he was gripping his little moose toy, and I grabbed his wrist….I pulled…dragging him to me….I saw his terrified face streaked with soot, his eyes bulging white, when my heart stopped….My hand held only air….Danny was jerked from me, dragged back into the seething inferno…. No….Someone was pulling him away from me….No….I had him and I lost him.

Now Wyatt was inching closer to finding Danny, with every grain of new information—McDade's photo, his attempt to find his son on the dark web, the connection to California. *And, my God, a homicide.*

Wyatt didn't care if it was getting dangerous.

I've already lost my wife. I can't lose my son again.

Wyatt was so absorbed he nearly didn't hear the call for his stop; the 63rd Drive–Rego Park station. He got off and walked a few blocks to Jane Dobson's home to pick up Molly. After thanking and paying Dobson, Wyatt walked with Molly through Rego Park, where the hickory and oak trees shaded the small, neat yards of postwar homes. Arriving at his frame house, he got food and water for Molly.

He was set to eat some cold leftover pizza, but had no appetite. He went to Danny's room, sat on his bed, running his fingers over Danny's toy moose, its blackened body, turning over the marble base to again read the words *Danny Wyatt, Banff Canada.*

This had been in Danny's hand. This had survived.

Molly appeared, and nuzzled Wyatt's leg. He stroked her head, as his phone vibrated with a message.

Agnes Finney on the desk.

He closed his eyes for a moment, exhaled, then set the moose back.

Deciding to respond from his laptop, he went to his desk, opened the computer, and logged into True Signal. He read Finney's message, asking if he had anything for the story Sked.

He typed, "Nothing from me today, Agnes."

She wrote back, "Thanks."

No commentary this time, Agnes? Wyatt shrugged. Then, since he was in the system, he decided to look at the updated Sked to see what other reporters had going, scrolling through the entries. Many were still ongoing.

HOSTAGEHUNT, by Denis Hugo, PARIS: Dragnet across Europe for bank robbers who fled with three bank tellers. LOSTEMBRYOS, by Sylvia Parker, CHICAGO: Eggs and embryos lost after storage failure at fertility clinic. JETMYSTERY, by Ana Ilano, MANILA: Families search for answers a year after jetliner disaster.

He continued scrolling through the long list, feeling Molly's head on his lap, petting her ears when he came to:

MURDERADOPTION, by Sabrena Roha, LOS ANGELES: The murder of a retired California librarian upon her return from Mexico may be linked to an illegal global adoption network. (Developing; may require travel.)

"What the —!"

He sat upright with such suddenness, he caused Molly to bark.

Wyatt cursed, and Molly barked again.

"Shh." He calmed her. "I don't believe this!"

Reading it again, letting it sink in. His mind racing, he reasoned how this fit with what McDade had told him, with what DeCastilla had told him.

This is it! Sabrena Roha is on this story!

Keyboard clicking, Wyatt got into True Signal's staff directory, finding then calling Roha's number.

It rang twice before she answered. "Sabrena Roha."

"Hi, Sabrena. Ray Wyatt, True Signal in New York."

"Hi, Ray."

"I don't think we've ever met since I joined."

"No, but I know your work. What you did on the Hydra in Vermont was outstanding."

"Thanks. Your work is stellar, too, but the Hydra is why I'm calling. I just saw your Sked entry. I think you're onto something that's tied to the Hydra."

"Really? What's that?"

"Is what you have exclusive?"

"Yes, so far."

"Listen, are you planning to file soon?"

"No, I need to do more work."

"Sabrena, I need you to tell me all you know on this."

A moment passed.

"Why, Ray? What's going on?"

"I think my son was taken into the adoption ring and is still being held."

PART TWO

CHAPTER 23

Guatemala City, Guatemala

A few weeks before Wanda Stroud was murdered in California, Cristina Yaqui woke before dawn.

Her small, immaculate stucco house was in a poor neighborhood, far from the *zonas rojas*. But not as far as she would've liked, because the reach of gangs was long, and Cristina worried that Samuel, her 14-year-old nephew, was being targeted for recruitment.

Cristina rose from her bed while Samuel slept. Keeping the light low, she washed, dressed, made Samuel his breakfast, kissed his forehead, and left for work.

Shouldering her bag, walking to the main street to wait for her ride, Cristina took some comfort in knowing Reyna, her neighbor, would soon collect Samuel. Reyna would see that Samuel, and her son, Chano, headed off to school, despite Samuel's protests to Cristina.

"I'm not a baby. I don't need Reyna. I can handle myself."

It saddened Cristina. Yes, soon Samuel would be a man, but his anger was hardening him, leading him down the wrong path. Cristina understood, but her fear for him was growing. Samuel's mother, Cristina's older sister, had died after she was struck by a bus four years ago. A year later, Samuel's father left for the U.S. border and a better life, promising to send for him. But he was robbed and killed in Mexico.

Cristina lived alone and took in her orphaned nephew.

They were the only family left for each other.

Now, standing in the darkness waiting for her ride, the still air filling with the aroma of cooking, and the traffic sounds of the waking metropolis, Cristina reflected on her life.

Unlike her late sister, who had left their village in the north for the excitement of the city, Cristina stayed behind. Then the earthquake and mudslide destroyed everything, killing their parents.

At her sister's urging, Cristina came to the city. She got married, but her husband was an abusive alcoholic. She left him. Cristina's only baby, a girl, was stillborn. She had no other children. After leaving her husband, Cristina followed her sister's advice—she went to the food market, and offered herself as a maid to work for the rich women in the suburbs.

This has been her life for years.

Cristina saved her money, and rented a small house. She planned to earn enough for her and Samuel to go to America or Canada.

This was her dream.

A pair of headlights slowed near the curbside; brakes creaked. A pickup truck with many dents in it, tools and building materials in the back, stopped. The passenger door opened.

Abril, Cristina's friend, slid closer to her uncle, the driver, as Cristina got in. With the usual morning greetings, Abril passed Cristina a thermos of coffee. They continued across the city, with the uncle squinting into the horizon. Dawn was breaking.

Abril's uncle, Juan, was a contractor, who helped repair and build houses in the wealthier neighborhoods where Abril, like Cristina, was employed. At Abril's insistence, Juan agreed to give Cristina a ride to her job every morning because he worked in the same area as the families Abril and Cristina worked for.

As they drove, Cristina looked out at the city, remembering her life in her village before the earthquake and the mudslides. She remembered the hands and faces of her mother and father among the dead, reaching up from the dried mud in which their bodies were entombed.

Cutting across the city, they began climbing the roads that curved up the hillsides of Zone 15 to the big houses of wealthy families. Juan slowed, and then stopped in a twisty, terraced section shaded by palms and shrubs.

This was a secluded part of the zone—a tranquil, dignified corner with little crime, where little happened. The houses here were partially visible from the road, beyond the flora, the steel-tipped white privacy walls, and metal gates. They were fortified with razor wire, and security cameras. Access was gained through a security gate intercom keypad.

Cristina and Abril got out and waved to Juan as he drove off.

The houses they worked in were near each other. It's how they met.

Before the two women parted for the day, they turned to see an unfamiliar car; it looked new. It had stopped at the security post outside the metal gates of the big white house across the street.

In the quiet, they heard the driver's power window lower, and a man's voice speaking into the intercom. They couldn't understand him, but knew he was an English-speaking foreigner. A woman sat in the front with him. She glanced quickly at the neighborhood through her dark glasses.

With an electronic buzz, a clang, and then humming, the gates opened, and the car advanced along the driveway. The gates closed, locking behind it.

"Another one, and so early this time," Abril said. "Foreigners are always coming and going at that house."

"What do you think is going on there?"
"Who knows?"

CHAPTER 24

Guatemala City, Guatemala

Selecting a colorful huipil blouse and holding it against her front, the woman turned, modeling it for the man with her as they shopped in the Mercado Central.

"I love this embroidered design," she said. "I'm getting it."

She passed the top to the woman in the stall, slipped off her backpack, undid its buckles, and withdrew her wallet. After paying, she put her folded new top and wallet in her backpack, and slid it back on.

The couple continued down the narrow walkway, browsing the stalls, their shelves, and tables, jammed and overflowing with T-shirts, sandals, handcrafted figurines, artwork, and display cases with jewelry.

Samuel followed them, careful to keep a safe distance.

He knew by the way they were dressed and how they talked that they were English-speaking tourists. Maybe from Australia, Canada, England, or the U.S. It didn't matter. Being tourists meant they were rich, and Samuel had locked onto the woman's wallet in her backpack.

He was going to take it.

But not here. Not yet.

Today was Samuel's initiation test, Normande, a crew leader, had told him. For Samuel to prove he had what it took to be admitted to Normande's gang, one of the most notorious of La Limonada, he had to deliver to Normande a wallet from a tourist today. Then Normande, whose arms were sleeved with tattoos, touched a spot on Samuel's clear arm where his success and acceptance would be celebrated with his first official gang tattoo.

Samuel's test to join the gang meant he had to feign illness, miss class, and lie, saying his aunt was coming for him while he slipped away from the inattentive staff at the school. Only Chano knew what was up, and he covered for his friend, swearing to the teachers that he had seen Samuel go home with his aunt.

After walking out of his school, Samuel made his way downtown to Zone 1. At the bustling plaza, he hunted for a target. Spotting a couple among the many tourists was easy. He took interest in a man with a red shirt and the woman, in a white shirt, accompanying him. Samuel concentrated on the woman's small, white leather backpack.

Ripe for the taking.

He had followed them as they strolled around the cathedral and down into the busy Mercado Central, waiting for the right time.

Building his courage.

This was his chance to join the gang, which he wanted more than anything. The gang would be his true family. God had killed his mother and father. God had abandoned him. Cristina didn't understand. She seemed to embrace her fate to clean toilets for the rich for the rest of her life. With a gang, Samuel would be somebody— somebody respected, somebody feared. Part of a force with the power to take what life owed him.

Today, it was a foreigner's wallet.

Today was his shot to prove he was a hard-core gangster, and he didn't want to blow it.

Samuel's heart was beating faster now as he stalked the couple, waiting for the right time. The Mercado was too confined; he could easily be trapped.

Be patient.

Eventually, the couple returned to the street, and Samuel remembered his training from Paulo, a gang expert in the art of stealing from tourists.

"With this type of backpack, you wait for a crowd."

Paulo had a gang member put on a backpack to demonstrate.

"You must bump into them from the back. Instinctively, they'll step away. But you clasp it here, and with your knife—which must be razor-sharp—you cut the straps here and here. Pull quick and hard, like this. See, it comes right off before they react. You must strike like lightning, then run like the wind, disappear in the crowd."

Having left the Mercado, the couple walked along the pedestrian street, browsing the vendor stalls. They checked out the food tables with bunches of radishes, onions, and celery. They looked over the tables where artisans were selling handmade pieces.

Samuel saw an increased flow of people approaching as the woman stopped, and leaned over a display of candles. Taking an interest, she was pointing and asking questions of the vendor. The man yawned while scrolling through his phone as people streamed past them.

Samuel slid his hand into his pocket, feeling the knife. Paulo showed him how to use the switchblade. People were passing by the couple in both directions as he neared them.

Do it now.

Gripping the knife the way Paulo showed him, Samuel's pulse quickened.

Scanning the flow of people, he held his breath. Holding his knife, hand at his side, strategically timing it, he intentionally bumped into strangers, and then bounced against the woman. She stepped forward, while he steadied himself by grasping her backpack. Pressing the knife's button, the blade opened; he sliced the leather

REQUIEM

straps, pulling fast and hard, feeling the backpack come free. The woman reached in vain at the straps in front.

Turning, she shouted, "Hey!"

But no one was there, and her backpack was gone.

Samuel was a dozen steps away, clutching the backpack, threading through the crowd at top speed.

"Tim, he's got my backpack, my wallet, my passport!"

Samuel glanced back. The man in the red shirt had started after him.

Samuel was running hard, and the knife had slipped from his hand. In his excitement, he'd sliced his fingers. Blood webbed along his hand and arms as he weaved around benches and trees.

Leaving the street, he came to the honking horns, the hum and growl of traffic. His heart thumped as he ran past the parked motorcycles and across the plaza.

Samuel continued running as fast as he could, but the red-shirted man must have been some kind of athlete.

He's gaining on me.

Samuel raced down the streets, slipped into an alley, and ran down the stinking, trash-filled back lanes. His throat ached from breathing hard.

Eyeing a fence nearly hidden by shrubs, Samuel headed for it.

This could be his escape.

Samuel began climbing, his heart slamming against his ribs, his hand bleeding as he neared the top. He threw one leg over, straddling, preparing to slide to freedom, when something seized his ankle.

CHAPTER 25

Guatemala City, Guatemala

Cristina began her workday at the big house in the hills by making breakfast for the *señor*, the *señora*, and their son and daughter.

The *señor* thanked Cristina "for another fine meal," and then left for his office in one of the skyscrapers downtown. The *señora* drove the children to their private school after giving Cristina her day's instructions. Today, she had very few, leaving Cristina to her regular duties.

Cristina cleaned up the kitchen, and then began the laundry. Making up the family's bedrooms, she started in the *señor* and *señora*'s room, with its grand bed, fitting for a king and queen. The boy was 10, and his room, as large as Cristina's house, had posters of his football heroes. His sister was 13, and in her room, she had pinups of pop stars she adored.

While in the girl's room, Cristina would think of her lost child, imagining the kind of daughter she'd be now if she'd lived. Cristina would be overwhelmed with bittersweet feelings, entangled in her worry for Samuel. Life with a daughter would be no less hard for them, but she imagined how wonderful it would have been to be a mother, to watch her child grow, and maybe find a better life.

Today, the *señora* had informed Cristina that she had appointments all day. So, Cristina made a light lunch of chicken, cheese, and tortillas. As required, she ate at the small table in the alcove in the kitchen with Santiago, the gardener, who also took care of the pool. He was older, and had a hunched back. Santiago said very little, but was good at his job.

Before resuming her work, Cristina put out some food and milk for Quito, the family cat, who often patrolled the property chasing butterflies or hunting mice.

Cristina then walked around the pool to the edge of the property, taking in its commanding view of the city below from the hills. No matter how many times she looked, it remained breathtaking.

The afternoon flew by, with Cristina scrubbing floors and cleaning bathrooms. She finished as the *señora* arrived home with her children. The children chattered on to Cristina about their friends as she made a snack they loved—sliced green mango, with chili and lime, just like the ones sold from street carts. She also ensured all was ready for the evening meal before Marco, the family's chef, and another girl came for their shift.

Later, with her day done, the *señora* thanked Cristina. She left, walking out the gate to the grassy slopes of the street. Abril was sitting under the shade of a palm in the spot where they waited for Juan.

The two women talked while looking at the gated walls of the house across the street. Cristina took out her phone, which the *señora* had purchased for her long ago. The *señora* paid for it because she wanted to keep in touch with Cristina, to alert each other if she couldn't come in, or to any special duties. The *señora* said the phone was like a gift Cristina could use personally, just as long as the *señora* could always reach her.

Cristina didn't know many people who had phones, but she liked taking pictures with hers. Now she was showing Abril her latest.

"Here's one of Samuel," she said.

Abril beamed at it. "He's becoming a young man so fast."

"Yes." Cristina stared at him for some time before swiping. "And here's one of a parrot I saw in the garden. So pretty."

At that moment, they watched a new stranger's sedan ease up to the gate of the house across the street. Abril grasped Cristina's arm.

"Take a picture of them!" Abril said.

"Why?"

"They could be celebrities!"

"That's silly. You think so?"

"Hurry."

From their vantage point in the shade, they were nearly concealed by the shrubs. Cristina raised her phone, zoomed in with the focus on the car. She took a photo, then another showing the car and house. She took more as the driver, a foreigner, leaned to the security post, and spoke into the intercom. The gate clanged open, swallowing the car.

Cristina showed Abril the pictures.

"What if it's a famous movie star?" Abril said.

"Why would it be a movie star?"

"I don't know." Abril shrugged, smiled, and then said, "But seriously, Cristina, something's going on at that place. Often, I see a car go in, usually only with a man and a woman. But when they leave, they have a young child with them."

"So, maybe it's a school for diplomats' children, or a babysitting service?"

"Maybe yes, maybe no," Abril said.

At that instant, the door in the wall of the house opened, and a woman walked out quickly, her hands flying to her face.

She had crossed the street, heading to walk right past them. As she neared, they heard her crying. She was about their age, and was dressed as if she worked there. Cristina and Abril exchanged looks of concern. Then Abril stepped out of the shade.

"*Señorita*, please—" Abril held out her hand "—tell us what's wrong, come and sit with us."

Startled, the woman looked at Abril, then Cristina.

"It's okay," Cristina said. "We work in the houses here. Do you work at that house?"

The woman didn't answer, but she didn't move.

"We're just waiting for our ride," Cristina said, gesturing for the girl to join them in the shade, which offered some privacy. "Come talk to us."

The girl hesitated before joining them under the tree.

"Are you going somewhere? We can give you a ride in my uncle's truck," Abril said. "Tell us what's wrong."

In the shade, the woman watched the house for a long moment, deciding whether she should speak, then said, "I've been let go."

"Why?"

"They just said they don't need me anymore." She kept her eyes on the house. "I have to go."

"Wait," Cristina said. "Why do so many cars come and go at the house?"

The girl stared at Cristina without answering. They all looked down the road as the rumble of Juan's pickup sounded. His battered truck crested the hill, and creaked to a stop before the women.

Seeing the truck, the girl said, "I should go."

"No, ride with us," Abril said. "Tell us what's happened." Then she opened the passenger door. "We're going to give this girl a ride, too."

Juan, exhausted from a day of working in the sun, rolled his shoulders and dragged the back of his arm across his forehead. The women crammed into the cab, with the girl sitting between Abril and Cristina, who could feel the girl's body trembling against hers.

Cristina glanced back at the house as they pulled away.

By the time they were out of the hills, the girl began telling them what she knew about the house.

CHAPTER 26

Guatemala City, Guatemala

Cristina arrived home, not sure of what to make of the story the girl had told her and Abril about the house where she had worked.

Or if it was true.

Clearly the girl was rattled.

She struck them as being a simple country girl. She didn't want to tell them her name, or the name of her employer, pleading with Cristina and Abril after she'd finished to never repeat the story she'd told them.

"I shouldn't have spoken about it," she'd said, wiping her tears, urging them to forget her babbling. She said the people at the house had given her a generous bonus, and that she was returning to her town in the mountains.

At her insistence, they let her out at a Transmetro station, where she disappeared, like the wisp of a dream.

Strange. All very strange.

Cristina's thoughts shifted when she got home and opened her door, ready to make dinner for her and Samuel. She had rice and chicken.

But Samuel was not home.

She took stock of her empty house, then left.

A few minutes later, she was at Reyna's house, knocking on her door.

"Hi, Cristina," Reyna said.

"I'm here for Samuel."

"He's not here."

"Didn't he come here with Chano after school?"

"I don't think so." Reyna called to her son. "Chano!" He came to the door. "Did Samuel come home from school with you before I got home?"

His eyes flicked from his mother to Cristina.

"No. He said he was sick, and that Cristina was taking him home."

"This is the first I heard of this," Cristina said. "I never went to the school. The school never notified me." She reached into her bag for her phone. "I'll call them."

Cristina took a moment to find the number, tapped the phone to make the call. After several rings, it was answered with a recorded message.

"They're closed now," Cristina said. She turned to Chano. "Did he talk to you? Did he say anything?"

Chano's face tensed as he shook his head.

"Chano," Cristina said. "Was he really sick? Is there something you're not telling me?"

At that moment, Cristina's phone rang in her hand.

Startled because she rarely received calls, her finger found the button to accept the call.

"Hello?"

"Señorita Cristina Yaqui?" a man asked.

"Yes."

"This is Detective Sebastian Cruz, with the PNC. Is Samuel Yaqui, aged fourteen, your nephew?"

Cristina's heart skipped. She swallowed.

"Yes."

"Are you his guardian?"

"Yes. Yes, what's happened?"

"He's been arrested for—"

"Arrested?"

"For stealing a woman's bag in Centro today. He's in custody. I need you to sign some papers. Could you come to my office in Zone 1 as soon as possible? I'll direct you on where to go."

**

Cristina had never set foot in a police station before.

Fighting tears, she followed the detective's instructions when she entered the lobby. She gave her information to the female officer at the desk, who told her to sit in the waiting area.

She closed her eyes for a long moment, praying for everything to be sorted so she could bring Samuel home.

Amid shouting and scuffling, she saw a man, cursing, slurring, and staggering, his hands handcuffed behind his back. His leg brushed hers as he was escorted past by two officers. Then two more officers went by, escorting a second handcuffed man, his face bleeding and his torn shirt bloodstained. Cristina's mind erupted with a new wave of worry at Samuel being in this place.

"*Señorita* Cristina Yaqui?"

Standing before her was a man in his 30s with very short hair. He had on a white shirt, jeans, ID hanging from his neck, and a gun in his shoulder holster.

"Yes."

"Detective Sebastian Cruz. This way."

They went up two flights of stairs, to an area with an open floor plan and an array of glass cubicles and desks. He led her to his desk and pulled out a visitor's chair for her. A framed picture of Cruz, smiling, with a pretty woman and a young boy and girl, was next to his computer. He took up a file folder.

"I need to confirm your identification."

Cristina presented her identity card. He studied it, took down the number, returned it, and then began relating events.

"Samuel has been charged with stealing a woman's bag, with her wallet and passport, today near the Mercado Central. He was chased and caught by her husband, a British police officer. They are tourists on vacation."

Cristina covered her mouth with her hand.

"This is very serious. We believe what Samuel did is part of a gang initiation. I work in the gang unit. We don't yet know which gang, because he refuses to cooperate with us."

Cristina shook her head slowly.

"We'll hold him here overnight. He's to appear in court tomorrow, or the next day, to enter a plea, and for the judge to determine a trial date and conditions. He could be sent to Las Gaviotas until his case is cleared."

"Las Gaviotas?"

"Yes. While this is Samuel's first offence, anything gang-related will be looked at with all seriousness by the courts. Can you read, and can you write your name?"

She nodded, and he opened the file folder with documents requiring her signature. She tried to read, but her tears blurred her vision.

"This is to say that as guardian, you're responsible for him, and you've been informed of the charges and the process," he said.

She signed.

"May I see him?"

Cruz closed the folder.

"I'm sorry, not tonight." He wrote on a piece of paper, and then passed it to her. "The top number is mine, if you need to reach me. The next is the number and address for Karen Ceto, the public defender attached to Samuel's case. She is to be in court with him tomorrow. You may see her tomorrow morning, and discuss the matter further with her."

Cruz paused. "I'll come to the point. My interest is for Samuel to provide us information about the senior gang members who are behind this. Stealing wallets and passports is very serious, because some of these gangs work for the big cartels."

Cristina nodded.

Cruz escorted her to the lobby, where he touched her shoulder.

"Remember," Cruz said. "If Samuel helps us, we can help him."

Cristina left, leaning her back against the building. She remained that way in the street—thinking nothing, feeling nothing.

CHAPTER 27

Guatemala City, Guatemala

Alone at home that night, Cristina couldn't sleep.

In the darkness, she looked from her bed through the open door to Samuel's room. Not seeing him in his bed unleashed a torrent of images, starting with the drunken, bloodied men at the police station; then the images of her mother and father, half buried in the mud; memories of her sister; the loss of her baby.

I can't lose Samuel. He's all I have left.

Thinking of him in jail, her fears gnawed at her the way the half-starved, snarling dogs gnawed on bones in the alley, tormenting her until she rose at her usual time. She followed her routine, keeping the light low. Washing and dressing, she started Samuel's breakfast before catching herself and stopping. In the predawn, she walked to the main street to wait for her ride. When Juan's pickup truck pulled over, she went to the open door, but didn't get in.

"I can't ride with you today. I have to take care of something."

"What's wrong?" Abril asked.

"It's a family thing with Samuel. Maybe I'll see you tomorrow."

"Is everything okay?"

"I'll know more after today."

Abril couldn't read Cristina's face in the dark, but sensing worry in her tone, she reached out for Cristina's hand.

"Good luck," Abril said, letting her hand slip as she and Juan drove off.

At home, Cristina cleaned her house; it was already clean, but it kept her busy. Afterward, she washed again, dressed in her best clothes and fixed her hair. When the time was appropriate, she called the *señora*.

"Please forgive me, but I can't come to work today. My nephew is not—" she had to find the words "—he's not doing so well."

A silence passed.

"Oh no. Cristina, I'm sorry. Is it something serious?" the *señora* asked.

"I'm not sure. But I may need to be away a couple of days."

"Of course. If we can help, let me know. Thank you for calling. Keep me updated."

It was not a lie, but it was close to one, and Cristina's stomach tensed at the deception.

Then she called Samuel's school, got through to someone at the office, and reported that he was ill and would be out of school for a few days. The school clerk noted his absence. The call ended, leaving Cristina feeling guilty for lying as she headed downtown to the public defender's office.

***

It was early when Cristina arrived. She waited in line outside with many others for more than an hour, until the staff began arriving and the doors opened.

The reception area became chaotic. When Cristina went to the front desk and requested to meet with Karen Ceto, the lawyer handling Samuel's case, the clerk checked her computer and then snapped, "I don't see your name. Do you have an appointment?"

"No. I only learned late yesterday about my nephew's arrest. Please, I need to speak with her."

"*Señora* Ceto's very busy. She has to be in court soon. You're supposed to make an appointment. Sit down. I'll call her."

Cristina returned to her seat, but someone had taken it, so she stood.

Waiting, she worried she might not be able to see the lawyer. Then she thought what if things got worse for Samuel, and the *señor* and *señora* learned the truth about his crime? It would be a reflection on her.

I could lose my job.

She didn't know how long she'd been grappling with her uneasiness when she heard her name.

"Yaqui!" A man, his face taut, was holding a piece of paper and looking at the people in the reception area. He repeated, "Cristina Yaqui for Karen Ceto!"

Cristina went with him to the second floor. Without speaking, he led her to a corner, where a woman in a nice blazer was seated behind a desk and on the phone. Her desk was pushed up against a window. The wall had file cabinets, bookshelves jammed with colored folders of case files, and her framed university degrees. Finished with her call, she extended her hand and welcomed Cristina to the chair beside her desk.

"I'm Karen Ceto. I'm afraid I don't have much time to discuss the case of—" she opened a folder and looked inside "—your son—"

"Nephew."

"Yes, nephew. Samuel Yaqui."

"I only wish to bring him home."

Ceto smiled.

"You spoke with Detective Cruz?"

"Yes."

"Look, the process is not so simple, and my caseload is heavy. Your nephew will appear in court later today. I'll ask for his plea to be set over to tomorrow, so I may have time to study his case further. I'll seek his release to your custody, but—"

"Oh, thank you, *Señora* Ceto!"

Ceto held up a palm.

"But we likely won't get it. So, he'll stay in holding."

"I don't understand."

"I spoke with him briefly last night about the crime he is charged with. I need to see the prosecutor's case file. I will urge Samuel to enter a guilty plea, and seek a suspended sentence because this is his first offence."

Cristina nodded.

"However, because police insist this involves gangs, it's very serious. They want him to give them names, which may lead to cartels because they want bigger fish. But he refuses. Cristina, if he cooperated with police and gave them names, it could help me press for a lighter sentence—even suspension—to keep him out of Las Gaviotas. That's a bad place for anyone, especially someone like Samuel. You understand what I am saying?"

"Yes. You need him to cooperate."

"Exactly." Ceto glanced at the clock on the wall. "I must go. "Do you have a phone?"

"Yes."

"Give me your number."

Cristina gave it to her.

"I'll call after I arrange with Detective Cruz for you to see Samuel this afternoon after court. Until then, you can see him appear briefly in court, in custody. Look for his name on the docket for the room number."

Ceto began placing files into her briefcase, signaling an end to their meeting.

"Thank you, *Señora* Ceto." Cristina stood. "Thank you."

CHAPTER 28

Guatemala City, Guatemala

Later that day, Cristina rubbed her temples while sitting at a table in an empty room at the police station, waiting to see Samuel.

Earlier, she had attempted to get a glimpse of him at court. But she'd misread the docket and went to the wrong courtroom. When she'd realized her mistake, it was too late.

His case had already been heard.

Samuel was gone.

But Karen Ceto was there, dealing with other clients and other cases. When Ceto finished and collected her files, Cristina approached.

"Hello again, Cristina," Ceto said.

"I missed seeing Samuel in court. I went to the wrong room."

"Let's talk outside."

They sat on a bench in the hall where Ceto touched her shoulder.

"I'm sorry to give you bad news."

"What's happened?"

"The prosecutor has given serious weight to Samuel's case. The British Embassy has expressed its concern because the victim is a British subject, the wife of a British police officer. They have connections."

"What does this mean?"

"It will make it difficult for us to obtain a suspended sentence and quick release. Also, the court is backlogged, and Samuel's case has been set over for two weeks for him to enter a plea then."

"Two weeks? But can I bring him home?"

"No. I'm sorry."

"Oh no," Cristina said. "So, he'll spend two weeks in Las Gaviotas? Two weeks with young men who are killers, gangsters, and rapists?"

Ceto shook her head. "I got the judge to agree that he be kept in the juvenile holding cells at the police station. It's safer for him there."

Cristina blinked back tears.

"And," Ceto said. "I've spoken to the prosecution and Detective Cruz. It's arranged for you to see Samuel later today at the police station."

"Thank you."

"Remember, there is hope for Samuel if he cooperates with police. Tell Samuel that, Cristina."

Now, sitting in the room rubbing her temples, a tissue clenched in her hand, Cristina's attention shot to the door as it opened.

Samuel entered with Detective Cruz.

Cristina gasped. Samuel's hair was messed. He looked gaunt, with bloodied cuts on his cheeks and lower jaw. His wrists were handcuffed in front of him. Cruz pulled out a chair for Samuel to sit across from Cristina, and then locked his handcuffs to the metal ring bolted to the table. Caressing the backs of Samuel's hands, Cristina noticed his scraped knuckles.

Cruz remained standing, spreading his hands on the table, leaning in between Samuel and Cristina.

"Before I go," Cruz said to Samuel, "listen to me carefully. The road you're on has no exit. It will end in prison or death. This is the time to help yourself by helping us."

Samuel said nothing.

"You and your aunt will have fifteen minutes," Cruz said, before leaving and closing the door behind him.

Taking stock of Samuel's condition, Cristina's eyes glistened.

"Are you hurt?"

He didn't answer.

"Were you beaten?"

Samuel looked at her, then shook his head slightly.

"How did you get the cuts on your face?"

He shrugged.

"I'm trying to bring you home."

He said nothing.

"Samuel, everyone knows you stole to join a gang. Why did you do this?"

He pursed his lips, his face hardening into someone Cristina didn't recognize.

"With them, I'll have money, power, and a family."

"A family of criminals. We're a family, Samuel."

"They are respected. We have nothing. We are nothing. You clean toilets for rich people, people who fear my gang."

His words pierced her, because they carried truth.

But they also carried Samuel's bitterness toward God, for taking his mother and father, ripping away so much from him. Now, before her eyes, Cristina saw Samuel turning his life from the light. As Cruz said, he was now on a path with no exit, one that ended in death.

"Samuel, you know that I'm working and saving so we can go to America," she said. "Karen Ceto says your case is very serious, but if you give Cruz the information he needs, she can get you released and keep you out of prison."

His jaw muscles bunched.

"I'll never be a rat. Do you know what they do to rats?"

"Samuel, please, I beg you to cooperate. All Cruz wants are names. It will save you from Las Gaviotas."

He sneered.

"I'm not afraid to go there. It will be a badge of honor, proving I'm not a rat. I'll be tattooed and revered as a legend. My gang will protect me there. And when I get out, I'll have earned a higher rank."

His handcuffs clinked as Cristina took his hands in hers, tears rolling down her face while he looked coldly at the wall.

A long moment of silence. The door sounded and Cruz entered.

Time was up.

CHAPTER 29

Guatemala City, Guatemala

Minutes after failing to convince Samuel to cooperate, Cristina, overwhelmed by defeat, sat with Detective Cruz at his desk.

"Did you hear what I said, Cristina?" Staring at her, Cruz repeated, "Will Samuel provide us information?"

"He refuses." Her voice was a whisper.

"It's unfortunate." Cruz turned to his files. "Things are going to get rough for him when I inform the prosecutor. Given that the British government is interested in the outcome, there will be many ramifications."

Cristina was numb with fear of losing Samuel. Her chest tightened in desperation.

"Now," Cruz took up a pen. "As his aunt, you, Cristina Yaqui, are employed as a family maid in a house in Zone 15, correct?"

A house in Zone 15.

In that moment, a fiery glint of hope flashed in Cristina's mind, but the desperation crushing her chest hadn't loosened.

Samuel was slipping from her. She'd do anything to save him.

But should I—could I—do this?

Perhaps she could seek help from the *señor* and *señora*?

No, the admission of her nephew's gang affiliation would mean the end of Cristina's job, and make it impossible to get another one with another family. Besides, she was already creating a web of deception and lies with them and Samuel's school. Soon, more people will know the truth. She had no power, no influence, nothing with which to save Samuel.

Nothing but one piece of information.

But shouldn't she first go home, think it over? Possibly discuss it with Ceto or Reyna?

No, there was no time.

"Cristina?" Cruz looked at her. "You work as a family maid in a house in Zone 15, correct?"

In that moment, like an answered prayer, her hope to save Samuel emerged. Cristina sat up and turned to Cruz.

"You want information from Samuel to catch bigger fish?"

Cruz grinned.

"That's one way to put it. But yes, we're always looking for bigger fish."

"If you had information about possible criminal activity, something I provided, that was not related to him, could you still use it to help him?"

Cruz furrowed his brow.

"I'm not sure. What're you getting at?"

"A tip. If I gave you a tip about something, would it help my nephew?"

Cruz looked at her for a long moment.

"What is it that you know?"

CHAPTER 30

Guatemala City, Guatemala

Detective Cruz eyed Cristina with coolness.

She would not reveal the information she had unless Samuel's lawyer, Karen Ceto, was present.

It was late in the day, nearing the time when people usually went home.

But at Cristina's insistence, Cruz called Ceto who, after rescheduling appointments, agreed to see them at her offico.

Now, the three of them sat in a meeting room—Ceto, with a pen, and a yellow legal pad, and Cruz, with his arms folded, leaning back in his chair.

"Before I tell you," Cristina began, looking at Cruz, "I want you to assure me that in exchange for this information, you will tell the prosecution to release Samuel."

"That's not how things work," Cruz said. "If you know of a crime and refuse to report it, we may consider you a participant, and that could be bad for you."

"Hold on," Ceto said. "Cristina, tell us what you know. Then we can proceed."

"No one must know that what I'm going to tell you came from me, please," Cristina said.

"Go ahead," Cruz said. "What does this concern?"

"It concerns a house in Zone 15, near where I work, activities that I and—I and others—have witnessed."

"What activities?" Cruz asked.

Cristina related how she and others had watched the steady coming and going of several cars with foreigners, most all leaving with children. She recounted what the troubled girl had revealed during her ride after she had been let go—that the house had been operating as a "black market" adoption agency for unwanted babies and orphaned children; that nearly all of the parents adopting the children were foreigners who had paid massive amounts of money; that the children were smuggled to Central and South America, but ultimately taken to Europe, with authentic paperwork provided by the agency and bribes to government officials; and that upward of 70 children had been known to be kept in the house.

When Cristina finished, the room fell silent.

Ceto and Cruz traded glances.

"Do you have the names of the people operating this agency?" Cruz asked.

"No."

"Can you give me the address of the house?"

"Yes."

"Anything else you can provide?" Cruz said.

Cristina thought, then reached for her phone and shared with Cruz and Ceto photos of the sedan and occupants she'd taken at the entry gates of the house.

Ceto made notes while Cruz clenched his jaw, absorbing the magnitude of what Cristina had told them.

"You know, Detective," Ceto said, "Guatemala outlawed international adoptions years ago after international pressure. What Cristina is describing appears to be a major criminal operation with global aspects."

Cruz nodded.

"This has the potential," Ceto continued, "to be a very significant criminal case that goes well beyond a purse snatching in the market. This has worldwide implications. It's the type of case that can benefit a detective's career."

"If true," Cruz said. "We have to keep in mind the source of the information—" he nodded to Cristina "—and its context, before we investigate this alleged activity further."

"Interesting," Ceto said. "Let's say, hypothetically, the national press was to learn about this house in Zone 15. And let's say, again hypothetically, that the press also learned that police knew of the operation but did nothing, leaving it to journalists to uncover the alleged truth. It would likely draw the attention of international media. Let's consider that context and possible impact."

Gritting his teeth, Cruz tapped his fingers on the table and let out a breath.

"All right. I'll take this to my supervisors with a request to investigate."

"And push for Samuel's release," Cristina said.

"First," Cruz said, "let's see what the preliminary investigation yields."

"We'll be waiting and watching closely," Ceto said.

CHAPTER 31

Manhattan, New York

In the upper reaches of a 70-story glass tower on Manhattan's West Side, Chase Lockner, managing editor of True Signal News, looked into his computer monitor upon launching the video conference.

Video windows of Ray Wyatt, participating from his home in Queens, and Sabrena Roha, from her apartment in California, popped up on Lockner's screen. He activated the audio button.

"Everybody hear me?" Lockner said.

"Yes," Roha said.

"Got you," Wyatt said.

"I read your notes," Lockner said. "You guys want to double up on this story. All right, make your case. Ray, you start."

"This is the first time I'm telling you this, Chase, because I'd been working quietly on it before Sabrena's work came to light on the Sked."

Wyatt related how his sources had revealed what they'd discovered in the aftermath of the Hydra case, such as the killer's activities and the networks he associated with on the dark web.

"One thing they showed me was an image their experts believe is my son," Wyatt said.

"What?" Lockner said.

"As you know, I've never accepted Danny's death. I was stunned. I learned that the FBI, working with age-enhancing technology on other photos of him, is confident Danny's alive, that he was somehow taken into an illegal international adoption network."

"This is incredible, Ray," Lockner said. "Do you have these photos?"

"No, they would not let me copy them," Wyatt replied. "But a source then told me that the FBI's investigation into the network is connected to an active case in California—the homicide of a woman who'd just returned from Mexico. Then, when I saw Sabrena's entry on the Sked, I realized the two aspects were part of the same story. I'll pass it to her now."

"Sabrena, what do you have?" Lockner said.

"So, I talked with Ray last night, and I am one hundred percent convinced we're both on the same story."

Roha outlined all she knew about Wanda Stroud's disappearance and murder upon her return from Mexico City, going over all the key pieces she had from her sources. She noted that during the return flight, Stroud may have glimpsed something on the laptop of the man seated in front of her.

"From my sources," Roha said, "I have the man's name, José Luís Garcia. He's a lawyer in Honduras, who may be linked to very dangerous criminal organizations."

"Like cartels?"

"Most likely."

Lockner sat back, thinking.

"We need to pursue this, Chase," Wyatt said.

After a long moment, Lockner sat forward, steepled his fingers, and tapped the tips to his mouth. "This story stays with the three of us," he said. "We're going to remove Sabrena's entry on the Sked."

"I can do that with Agnes," Sabrena said.

"Yes. I want to keep this confidential, protect exclusivity," Lockner said. "Do you think anyone else knows what we know?"

"No," Wyatt said. "Not with my connection."

"And I haven't gotten a sense that anyone in L.A. is as deep into the Stroud case as we are at this point," Sabrena said.

"Ray, given this is your son, are you up to this? Do you see a conflict?"

"If you pull me off, I'll go after it freelance on my own dime."

"Yeah, I understand. Look, we could acknowledge your connection with a disclaimer at story time. But that's a bridge to cross. I am mindful we are talking about the life of your son and other children."

"That's right," Wyatt said.

"Chase, we've already seen one homicide in this so far," Roha said.

"Yes," Lockner said.

"So, what're you thinking?" Wyatt asked.

"I'll green-light this—travel, expenses, the usual. I'm putting you both on special assignment, reporting only to me. Go to Honduras, and track down José Luís Garcia. You're a couple researching adoption, making inquiries. You can say you've heard of his agency through the grapevine, that kind of thing. You can hire fixers— whoever and whatever it takes to pursue this to the end."

"What about our bureaus and stringers down there?" Roha asked. "Do we bring them into this?"

"Let's not, unless it's absolutely necessary," Lockner said. "I know you're both seasoned pros who've reported from Central America. You know what to do, but this could be dangerous. Are you up to it?"

"Absolutely," Roha said.

"Good. And you, Ray?"

"You know my answer."

"All right. Good work, both of you. Let's get going."

CHAPTER 32

Guatemala City, Guatemala

A few days after getting Cristina Yaqui's tip, Detective Sebastian Cruz was ensconced in a secluded spot of the terraced hillside, where the road curled above the beautiful properties of Zone 15.

Through binoculars, Cruz observed the house below. With those spear-tipped privacy walls, metal gates, razor wire, and security cameras, it was like a fortress. As were many of the houses in this area, it was shaded by palms, half-hidden by shrubs and thriving flower gardens.

A neighborhood fragrant with wealth, Cruz thought.

Occasionally he'd see a vehicle ease up to the security post outside the gate. An inaudible spurt of static and tin-sounding conversation were followed by the click and clang of the gate door rolling open. The sounds carried up to the unmarked Ford SUV where Cruz and his partner, Detective Pablo Pineda, were watching.

They were coming up on four hours now, and Pineda, who'd spent most of it with his face in his phone, groaned as he opened his door.

"We're wasting time. We've got other cases. I got to take a leak."

Pineda vanished into a dense clump of shrubs.

Cruz knew his partner's point was valid. He had been skeptical of Yaqui's tip that the place below was a house of illegal international adoptions, as Yaqui claimed. In fact, Cruz didn't believe her. He regarded her as a smart, fierce woman who'd offered the tip in a desperate act to save her nephew.

Let's face it. The kid was lost to gangs.

Still, Yaqui's information gnawed at Cruz, keeping him awake at night, distracting him at meetings.

He had to admit there were several underlying factors that had brought him and Pineda here, and several concerns. There was Ceto's threat to take Yaqui's information to the press; that alone was a potential nightmare. He hadn't yet advised his supervisors of what he was doing, telling his boss he and Pineda were checking a new "possible" lead on gang-cartel affiliations.

And there was the fact this area was home to diplomats, executives, people with wealth, power, and enough influence to make the life of a lowly detective quite ugly, even end his career.

But what if Yaqui's information was true?

In his heart, Cruz was a good cop. And a good cop follows all information, no matter where it comes from, no matter where it leads.

I just need to proceed carefully.

So, this morning, he signed out an unmarked car and took Pineda with him to observe this house, filling him in along the way.

The passenger door opened, and Pineda returned.

"Have any international criminals arrived, Sebastian?"

Cruz kept his binoculars focused on the house.

"I think," Pineda said, "you were fed a line by a woman protecting her nephew's ass. If anything, I bet this is a private, expensive childcare center for rich people, and nothing more."

"Perhaps, but we haven't dug into the property records for this address and the owners yet."

"Why not? Afraid you might step on some toes?" Pineda pointed to the city in the hazy distance. "We should be down there, chasing gangs. Not up here in the clouds, potentially pissing off the elites."

"You're the one who pissed in their bushes." Cruz continued, watching the house. "Have you noticed what's been going on down there, Pablo?"

"A few cars coming and going. So?"

"Each one we've seen go in has left with a child."

"So? Let's check childcare licenses. Like I said, childcare, babysitting."

"Perhaps childcare," Cruz said. "Perhaps something else."

CHAPTER 33

Munich, Germany

"For us, it's something we've desired for a long time," Hanna Beck, with her husband Deiter beside her, told their group.

More than a dozen people, their faces framed in small windows on their computer monitor, were listening.

"We've searched our hearts," Hanna said, "and given our situation, we accepted we could still be a family without experiencing pregnancy."

Deiter put his arm around her.

"While we won't have the joys of raising a baby from birth," Deiter said, "adopting an older child will come with its own joys. We're certain of that. And with the agency we're using, we're closer than ever to welcoming our new child into our home."

"Yes," Hanna said. "The waiting is almost over." She exchanged a teary smile with her husband.

"That's where we are at this point," Deiter said.

Their screen filled with the face of Penny Perkel, of the London-based adoptive parents' support group.

"That was lovely," said Perkel, who moderated the private online sessions. The group consisted of people at different stages in the process—ranging from those who'd completed adoptions, to those contemplating one.

They shared the dos and don'ts, the fears, the anguish, and the joys.

The participants were from around the world. They gave only their first names and their professions, making it a place where they were safe to speak from their hearts, where they received understanding, support, and help. The sessions were conducted in English, which all members spoke with different degrees of fluency.

"Thank you, Hanna and Deiter," Perkel said. "Now, to Marla and Gray in Boston."

"Hi, everyone." Marla waved. "We have news, too!"

Hanna and Deiter's monitor showed a man and woman in their early 40s. Marla had centered close to the camera a framed photo of a boy.

"As you know, this is Timur. He's five," Marla said. "Next month, we're going to Kazakhstan, to bring him home to be part of our family!"

Marla and Gray were both doctors who'd volunteered through an international humanitarian organization to provide medical care in war zones. It was how they met so many children like Timur, who was orphaned, surviving with aid groups in a refugee camp.

Marla and Gray had two biological children—a daughter, seven, and a son, nine.

"Timur needs a family," Gray said, "a chance at life, and we're thrilled and blessed that he'll become part of our family a few weeks from now."

Faint cheers of congratulations sounded.

Perkel returned to the screen.

"Wonderful," Perkel said. "We're celebrating with you and Timur. Thank you for that update. Now, I believe next, we'll go to Paris. Tamina, how are you doing? Do you wish to participate today?"

Hanna and Deiter's screen now displayed the face of a woman in her 40s. Over the woman's shoulder, through the large windows of her home, they could see the Champs-Élysées. Tamina, an art dealer, exuded an air of grace, even noblesse. Beside her was a framed photo of

Rasul, her six-year-old son, who had died suddenly three years ago of a brain tumor.

"Thank you, Penny." Tamina smiled, her eyes still sad. "Hello to everyone in the group." Tamina sighed. "Well, next month will be difficult for me with Rasul's birthday coming." She stopped, swallowed. "But speaking candidly with all of you like this helps me."

"That's why we're here," Perkel said.

Tamina nodded, pausing to choose her words.

"As those of you who've lost a baby, a child, know, you never stop loving that child. And while Rasul is gone, I still have mountains of love to give. Of course, I would do anything, or give anything in this world, to have Rasul back. But God has other plans. That is why I embarked on my adoption journey."

Hanna and Deiter watched, listening intently as Tamina took up her photo of Rasul, gazed at it, and then back to the camera. "I've been searching, wanting to adopt a son who has the same characteristics as Rasul. To give him the mountains and oceans of love I have. As you know, my search has been difficult and painful. My therapist continues to caution me. She says my reasons, while understandable, are emotional. I tell her I know, but it's *what my heart needs*."

Tamina set the photo down tenderly, composed herself, smiling to the camera.

"So, I keep searching, and with Heaven's help, I'll find a son."

Perkel returned to the screen.

"And our hearts are with you, Tamina," Perkel said. "We're here to support you on your journey."

A ripple of warm, compassionate approval sounded among the group.

"You're all very kind. Thank you," Tamina said.

Perkel said, "Next, we have Anthony and Eric in Vancouver."

Hanna and Deiter's screen showed the faces of two men in their 30s. They knew them from previous sessions. Anthony and Eric were teachers.

"We just want to say right off," Anthony said, "that our love goes out to you, Tamina."

"Yes," Eric said. "We're praying that it happens for you."

New murmurs of agreement rippled through the group.

"It was a long road for us before we adopted Lucas when he was six months old, and now he's three," Eric said. "And yesterday, we learned that we'll be adopting Li Na, from China, to be his baby sister. She's eight months."

"We're so fortunate to be adding to our family," Anthony said.

Gentle congratulations and cheers rose from the group. Perkel thanked Anthony and Eric before moving to other members. They shared their experiences, emotions, and tips before the session ended. Penny Perkel then wrapped it up by thanking everyone, and noting the date and time of their next session.

Hanna and Deiter's monitor switched to their screen saver, displaying a blue sky, palm trees, a white sand beach, and azure water.

Hanna found the sessions draining and released a long breath.

"Of all the support groups we're in," she said, "this is the most intense."

"It is." Deiter reached for his phone.

Staying in her thoughts, Hanna said, "So many people from different walks of life around the world, sharing the joys, and the heartbreak. Look at Tamina, in so much anguish. I'll send her another message from us, later."

Deiter was tapping and scrolling on his phone.

"Keep telling her that it's going to work out for her," he said, concentrating on his phone.

Hanna could see he was checking for updates from their agency.

"Any news?"

"Everything is in order. A few more months to go. We're doing this," Deiter said.

"Yes," Hanna said. "We're going to do this."

CHAPTER 34

Los Angeles, California

A strange feeling came over Jill McDade after landing at LAX.

Taking in the gates, the shops, lounges, and the bustle of passengers along the congested corridors, she imagined Wanda Stroud walking through this airport.

She had no way of knowing she was taking the last steps of her life.

Passing through the terminal somehow made the case more real for McDade, solidifying her determination to clear it and see justice done.

During the flight, she'd studied everything Special Agent Cal Banner had sent her—reports, statements, videos, and photos concerning Stroud's homicide. And McDade had sent him what they had on the Hydra and its aftermath. All of it underscored the magnitude of the growing investigation.

Now, in the cab to Westwood, gliding along L.A's freeways, she used the time to call Alison, who was staying with Gwen back home in New York.

"Can you bring me back a surprise present, Mom?"

"We'll see, honey. Be good. I love you."

"Love you, too."

"Let me talk to Gwen."

After a short chat, Gwen assured her, "Everything's fine here. Don't worry, Jill."

At her hotel, McDade checked in, freshened up, collected her things, and then got another cab to the FBI's office nearby on Wilshire.

After the perfunctory greetings and introductions, McDade, Banner, and a few other investigators went to a meeting room to work.

They began with McDade, connecting her laptop to a large flat screen at the end of the room. She pulled files from her bag, and then briefed the California team on all aspects of the Hydra investigation.

She explained that the Hydra case concerned a man using the alias Lasius Byyle. He had an online associate, Devlin Foxe, a realtor, who'd rented a secluded property to Byyle.

McDade's presentation included photos of Byyle, Foxe, and the secluded property. Investigators, in part with Foxe's cooperation, obtained screen shots from Byyle's activities on the dark web.

"Before proceeding on this aspect, we want to be clear," McDade said. "We don't suspect Byyle was involved directly in the illegal adoption network. But his online activities led us to these dark web networks and a major criminal operation. In his travels, Byyle floated into these networks, and that has enabled us to investigate further—to lift the rock, as it were, on children believed to be ensnared by an illegal adoption ring. This is some of what we found on Byyle's computer."

The large screen filled with the gallery of young faces, showing catalog numbers and prices.

"That's exactly what we got from Wanda Stroud from the plane," Banner said.

McDade continued, explaining how New York investigators were working with missing children's organizations and police around the world to identify children tied to the adoption ring by using age-progression and facial-recognition technology.

At the outset, they'd succeeded in identifying three children—a three-year-old boy from New York, who vanished in a hotel fire while on vacation with his family in Banff, Canada; a three-year-old girl, who'd vanished in Spain while with her father on the Madrid Metro; and a four-year-old British boy, who disappeared while with his family near the London Eye observation wheel in London.

"We've just identified two more children," McDade said. More images flashed up on the screen as she continued. They showed a two-year-old girl, missing from a grocery store parking lot in San Antonio, Texas, and a three-old-boy, who disappeared from his family in the Aricanduva Mall in São Paulo, Brazil.

McDade completed her update, leaving the images of the five children on the screen, to give the investigators a moment to process this facet of the case.

Banner then updated everyone on the status of the Stroud aspect. For McDade's benefit, he started at the beginning, also displaying photos, maps, and other records.

On the screen was a handsome white-haired man in his 50s.

"This is the man who was seated in the row ahead of Stroud, the man with the laptop. He is our suspect. His name, likely an alias, is José Luís Garcia, and we believe he is an attorney based in Honduras."

Banner went back, summarizing the case from Stroud's fateful walk through LAX, to her ride with Garcia, and finally to the place of her death in the rat-filled pit in San Pedro.

"Based on the facts and statements, we believe Garcia was careless on the plane. Stroud saw something she shouldn't have seen. Garcia and his people moved fast, killed her, and disposed of her phone. Fortunately for us, Stroud stored the evidence needed to solve her death online."

McDade and the others at the table nodded.

"The challenge is, Garcia and his people are experts at covering their tracks. Nothing on the car, or credit cards; anything that's surfaced was a stolen identity leading to a dead end. We don't know if Garcia's still in the country, or has fled. Bottom line—so far, they've vanished like ghosts."

McDade looked at a report in her folder, with the names Felix Neri, Victor Nyllev, and Alberto Aiza known to have been used by Garcia, along with a dozen other aliases. "I see Garcia uses passports from several countries, and has ten Social Security numbers," she said.

"That's right."

"Have we pursued all these names, run them down?"

"That is ongoing. We're attempting to determine if IDs were stolen online, or were a matter of lost wallets, stolen passports, or if they were completely fabricated."

"Any results?" McDade asked.

"So far, from our legal attaché at the U.S. Embassy in Tegucigalpa, Garcia in Honduras, the real José Luís Garcia reported his passport missing about a year ago."

"And we're satisfied with his response?" McDade said.

"It's been confirmed by Honduran authorities. We've yet to confirm anyone named José Luís Garcia is a lawyer in Honduras," Banner said. "We're still investigating."

"So, our subject could be using another alias," an investigator said.

"Do you know the circumstances of how the real José Luís Garcia of Honduras lost his passport?" McDade asked.

"Part of our ongoing investigation with our people and officials in Honduras," Banner said. "What we have are international criminals operating at a very high level of sophistication."

"Leaving us with no more than a fine thread into their illegal adoption network," McDade said.

"It could be operating anywhere in the world," Banner said. "We've issued alerts to our legal attachés at all U.S. Embassies, and this morning Interpol advised that they've approved our request to issue a Red Notice for

José Luís Garcia, or anyone using any of his aliases, passports, or Social Security numbers linked to our guy. For anyone who doesn't know, a Red Notice deems our subject a Wanted Person to be located and arrested on sight."

CHAPTER 35

Guatemala City, Guatemala

In the days after Cristina Yaqui had returned to her job at the big house in Zone 15, her worries continued burning like wildfire.

No one knew the anguish she carried for her nephew, Samuel.

He was still being kept in the juvenile holding cells at the police station, where, thank heaven, she was allowed to visit him. But he still refused to give police the names of gang members.

Karen Ceto, the public defender, had told her a backlog in the court had meant further delays for Samuel's case. Ceto was overwhelmed with other cases, and didn't know how much longer she'd be able to convince the court not to transfer Samuel to wait out his case in Las Gaviotas, where they kept hardened criminals.

And whenever Cristina had succeeded in reaching Detective Cruz to ask him about the house of illegal adoptions, his response was the same: "We're still looking into it."

Still, Ceto had said they must give Cruz a little more time in order to win favor and help Samuel.

With each passing hour, day and night, Cristina's fears deepened, because it seemed that nothing was happening.

So today, while cleaning, Cristina used every opportunity to glance out the windows toward the adoption house, not knowing what to expect.

Changing the sheets on the beds upstairs in the children's rooms, she looked out, down beyond the family's privacy walls and gate to the fortress that was the adoption house. But the angle and dense flora limited her view, and she craned her neck.

"Is everything all right, Cristina?"

She turned to see the *señora* in the doorway.

"Yes, *señora*."

"Because since your return, you appear distracted, even stressed. Is it Samuel, your nephew?"

"No, all is well."

"Because if there's anything you want to talk about, anything we can do, please tell me."

"Of course, *señora*."

The *señora* waited a moment, smiling, then said, "I'll have lunch by the pool, my usual. I need to do a little work there."

"Yes, *señora*."

It further anguished Cristina to not tell the family the truth about Samuel's arrest. But she believed it would result in her being fired, she thought later in the kitchen as she made the *señora* a fruit salad with nuts. She took the salad outside to the *señora*, who was at the table by the pool under the shade of the big umbrella, working on her laptop.

"Thank you. Oh, I forgot." The *señora* selected a cashew and crunched on it. "The children said Quito didn't come home yesterday."

"Yes. I have not seen him."

"Santiago told my husband he saw Quito go into the neighbor's yard, the one across and down the road. I guess he trotted in when the gate opened. That silly cat."

"Goodness."

"Would you go to their gate this afternoon and ask if you can go in, call Quito, or look for him?"

"The big white house down the street with all the security?"

"Yes."

Cristina hesitated, then smiled.

"Oh, *señora*, I'm sure Quito will return from his roaming."

"I know, but the children would be happy to see him sooner, rather than later. Go there, and tell the neighbors to call me if they have any questions. Give them my number."

"If you could call them first, *señora*, because I don't really know them."

"We don't know them, either." She selected another cashew. "I think they're leasing or renting. Maybe tourists, foreigners, I think. Don't be shy, Cristina. Take Quito's squeeze toy and call him. He'll jump into your arms."

Cristina didn't move.

The *señora* looked at her.

"Please, Cristina. It won't take long."

"Of course, *señora*."

CHAPTER 36

Guatemala City, Guatemala

Standing at the security post outside the gate of the white house, Cristina's finger shook, nearly missing when she pressed the intercom button.

Coming to this house, showing her face after reporting its activities to police, terrified her, and she clasped her hands together.

But no one knows me. No one knows who I am. Stay calm.

Her head swirled with apprehension as she listened to birdsong, and watched hummingbirds and butterflies flit among the flowers on the terrace before she heard static, followed by a tin-sounding male voice.

"Yes?"

Cristina cleared her throat and leaned closer to the speaker grill.

"Hello. I'm with the staff at a house nearby, and our cat has strayed onto your property. May I be permitted to come inside and collect him?"

Her request was followed with a long silence before it was broken.

"Wait."

After several minutes, a man walked down the driveway. Through the gate's metal bars, Cristina saw he was in his early 30s, with a muscular build and tattooed arms. He had thick hair, and a scar on his chin. His eyes were intense as they appraised her.

Cristina saw him register that she had a good figure and was reasonably pretty, affirming what her friends had said when they had encouraged her to find a boyfriend. Enjoying his assessment, he said, "You want to come inside and look for your cat?"

"Yes, please, if you'll permit me to look along the gardens."

His face was stone-cold.

"There are no cats here, *señorita*."

"We saw him slip inside. His name is Quito. He hides well when he's frightened, but will respond to his toy."

She withdrew the little red rubber ball with the bell inside from her pocket, held it up, squeezed it, and smiled.

The man thought.

"What is your name, *señorita*?"

"Cristina," she said with a smile.

"And you work nearby?"

"Yes."

Cristina tilted her head slightly. "And your name?"

"Me? I'm Manny."

Then Cristina saw his expression change into the beginnings of a shark's grin. As if agreeing with himself, he stepped to one side, pressed a button on a post. It was followed with an electronic buzz, a clank, then humming as the gates opened.

"You may take a quick look for your cat, *Señorita* Cristina."

Nodding her thanks, she stepped inside, then heard the gate close and lock behind her.

Cristina's pulse quickened.

Manny followed her as she searched the shrubs and gardens along the inside walls of the property. Some areas were deep, with overgrown entangled branches and vines making for small jungles.

"Quito. Quito," she called softly, squeezing the ball, jingling the bell, and clicking her tongue. "Quito."

Crouching at times to better examine the dense flora, Cristina noticed how Manny watched from behind while keeping a respectful distance.

The sudden squeal of young voices pulled Cristina's attention toward the house. A stream of children—all under five years old, including toddlers, and with caregivers pushing babies in strollers—flowed to the grassy play area.

Just as the girl told us!

Witnessing the children made it real for Cristina. Her heart racing, she resumed searching along the dense gardens along the privacy wall.

"Quito. Quito."

Keeping her voice soft, struggling to think, she worked her way closer to the house, where she had better views of several new cars parked in the circular driveway in front.

"No! As quickly as possible!" said a new male voice, deep with authority.

Glancing around for the source, Cristina scanned the house—a beautiful white stucco, with two stories and a red-clay tile roof. The upper level had a wraparound balcony, the windows and doors wide-open to catch breezes fingering from the shade of the tall palms.

"A problem in Los Angeles," the voice said. "Taken care of."

That's when Cristina spotted the speaker—a white-haired man in his 50s, wearing faded jeans and a navy polo shirt. He was of medium build; he looked fit—handsome, even. With a phone pressed to his ear, standing at the edge of the upper balcony, he turned to look down in Cristina's direction.

She turned to the garden and her search.

"Quito. Quito."

Cristina's heart pounded, fear exploding like fireworks. She didn't like being here, and wanted to leave when she heard purring.

A pair of eyes met hers from the foliage.

"Quito!"

The cat was nearly concealed by the fauna near the wall. Cristina began parting the massive leaves of plants, sweeping back branches to get to Quito.

As afraid as she was, Cristina was struck with a thought that could ultimately help Samuel.

Realizing she may never have this chance again, she reached for her phone. Scooping Quito into her arms, she used the cover of the thick vegetation to take photos of the children, the cars, the house, and the man, zooming in as close as possible before he vanished from the balcony.

"Did you find your cat?" Manny said.

Slipping her phone into her pocket, she emerged, holding Quito.

"Yes. Thank you, Manny." She glanced toward the children. "Such beautiful little angels. Is this childcare?"

"Something like that." He nodded to the driveway. "Time to go."

They started for the gate.

"Hey!"

They turned to see the white-haired man approaching, indicating Cristina. Breathing hard from apparently rushing, his face was taut.

"Who is this, Manny?"

"This is Cristina."

"The new girl? Here for an interview? We have a lot to do."

"No, no. She works at a neighbor's house. She came to collect her cat. He wandered into the yard."

Cristina stroked Quito.

The white-haired man eyed her.

"She found him, and now she's leaving," Manny said.

The white-haired man stared at her until his phone rang in his hand. He waved off Manny and Cristina, answered his call, and started back to the house.

Manny escorted Cristina and Quito to the gate and opened it for her.

Thanking Manny, she stepped to the street.

Quito meowed, squirming in protest until Cristina, her blood thundering in her ears, loosened her hold on him.

CHAPTER 37

Tegucigalpa, Honduras

Ray Wyatt stepped into the hotel elevator, heading down to meet Sabrena Roha for breakfast and to go over their plans.

As the car descended, he rubbed the back of his neck. He needed coffee.

Two days earlier, he had flown from New York to Houston, where he met Roha. She'd flown from Los Angeles. After staying overnight at the Holiday Inn near the airport, they took a direct flight together from Houston to Toncontín International Airport in Tegucigalpa.

Arriving yesterday in the late afternoon, they took a taxi to the Marriott in the business district on Juan Pablo II and checked into their rooms. With night falling, Wyatt, his laptop and notebook on his chest, studied his research. After reading everything, going online, and making notes, he opened photos of Lisa and Danny, loving their smiling faces. He could almost hear their laughter, almost touch them; almost feel them.

Almost.

Then he saw himself in the photos. *Like a ghost.* Because that part of him was gone, as if he'd lived another life with them.

He went to more pictures of Danny.

Danny as a baby in Lisa's arms.

Danny as a toddler when they went to Yankee Stadium.

Danny in the Rocky Mountains.

Danny just before the fire, pulling Wyatt back....

Crawling on his stomach...deeper into the choking smoke, calling Danny...his fingers finding Danny's hand...seeing his terrified face, his eyes bulging...But his hand held only air as something jerked Danny from him, pulling Danny back into the churning black clouds of the inferno....

Wyatt then stared at nothing.

What am I doing here in Honduras? Will I find Danny? Is it really him? What if McDade and the FBI are wrong? Will I ever see him again?

Wyatt turned to his hotel window, watching the lights twinkling from the hills surrounding Tegucigalpa.

Then he fell asleep.

That was last night.

Now, the elevator chime sounded for the main floor, shifting his concentration to real time.

Stepping off, Wyatt found the hotel restaurant, Cocina Latina, where there was a buffet breakfast. He savored the aromas of hot food and coffee, spotted Roha at a table, and gave her a small wave. Wyatt got scrambled eggs, sausage, hash browns, toast, and coffee before joining her.

A half-eaten muffin and yogurt were next to Roha's tablet. She was on her phone, talking softly in Spanish while Wyatt ate.

Ending her call, Roha got down to business.

"We've hit a snag," she said. "As we know, lawyers in Honduras cannot practice unless they are registered with the Honduran Bar Association."

"Right."

"The Bar Association tells me they have several members named Garcia, but no one named José Luís Garcia."

"Maybe he was suspended, disbarred, or let his membership lapse."

Roha shook her head, chewing some of her muffin.

"I asked them that," she said. "He was never registered. We could try law schools."

"Yes, and we have another possibility." Wyatt reached into his back pocket for his notebook, opened it to a page, and pointed to an underlined name. "Last night, I found a listing for a José Garcia, with Orchid Sea Consulting Group here in the city."

"Consulting?" Roha said. "That would fit, you know, if it's our guy."

"That's what I was thinking."

"Look at you," Roha said. "Thought you said your Spanish was weak."

Wyatt shrugged.

"I'm not fluent like you, Sabrena, but I covered a few stories in Central America back in the day. Maybe not as many as you with the *L.A. Times*, but I have a few sources and a few tricks."

Roha went online, finding Orchid Sea Consulting Group's website.

"Got it," she said.

"Call them. See if our Garcia works there."

Roha got on the phone. Soon she was talking softly in Spanish, asking for José Luís Garcia, stressing that she was searching for someone by that full name. A pause, then more Spanish, then she finished.

"Yes," she said. "A man named José Luís Garcia is with Orchid Sea, and he'll see us in one hour at his office for a confidential consulting matter."

"Good," Wyatt said.

They got together in the hotel lobby for their meeting. Roha sensed concern in Wyatt.

"Something's bothering you," she said.

"We've obtained Garcia's name as the man on the plane with Stroud, the man suspected to be involved in her murder, right?"

"Yes, absolutely."

"Well, the FBI would be all over him, so why would he be down here, agreeing to meet two strangers? It's too easy. Something doesn't feel right."

"Maybe we're one step ahead of the FBI," she said. "They've got bureaucracies to plow through."

"And maybe we've hit a dead end."

"Well, Ray, we won't know until we do the legwork. Let's get a taxi."

CHAPTER 38

Tegucigalpa, Honduras

Pulling away from the hotel, the taxi threaded through the traffic of the downtown business district.

Roha worked on her phone.

Wyatt took in the city.

Heading uphill, they made their way into what he guessed was Barrio Guadalupe, traveling along its serpentine roads, climbing and twisting up toward the next section. Moving along narrow streets, past laundromats, cafés, and cantinas, they came to residential areas, with cars parked behind steel security bars and high walls that fortified property.

A city of razor wire, he thought.

The walls of some buildings bore cracks, blisters, and stains from enduring hurricanes, earthquakes, and myriad stresses of a poor country. Still, Wyatt thought, the neighborhood looked no different than many in the U.S.

They reached Colonia Palmira, which stood in contrast to the impoverished areas. It exuded wealth, looking every bit like a modern suburb with its restaurants, boutiques, and embassies.

The taxi stopped at a new building, with curved architecture, wrapped in dark blue glass, and soaring 15 stories.

"This is it," Roha said, paying the driver.

The taxi drove off.

"So, we're not going to misrepresent ourselves," Roha said.

"Correct. We tell him we're researching adoptions, which is true."

"If it comes down to it, we play things by ear," she said. "And only if we feel we have to, do we identify ourselves as reporters who are interested in adoptions."

"Which is also true," Wyatt said.

"So, we're not married," she said. "But we're in a relationship, thinking of adopting. Our goal is to get inside their process, to document, record, and confirm all we can, to investigate ties to your son and Wanda Stroud's murder."

Wyatt looked up at the building.

"Think it'll work?" Roha said.

"No."

"Agreed."

"This would be much easier if we had a picture of the guy the FBI was looking for."

"Sure would."

"We'll be winging it all the way, Sabrena."

They entered and checked in with the guard at the reception desk. He reached for a phone. Several minutes later, a woman wearing a blazer and matching skirt arrived, and took them to Orchid Sea Consulting Group on the 10th floor.

Inside, she led them down a hall to the open double doors of a spacious office with a sweeping view. A man in a suit and tie rose from his desk; he was in his 50s, with thin white hair. He guided them to a sofa and chairs. They declined his offer of a beverage. He dismissed the woman, and she closed the doors behind her.

"Welcome, *Señora* Roha and—"

"*Señorita* Roha," she said, correcting him with a warm smile.

"*Señorita*." He returned the smile. "And *Señor* Wyatt. From America. Please, I am curious. How did you learn of our company?"

"From associates," Roha said.

"Ahh." He nodded, smiling with a measure of pride. "And what is the confidential project you wish to discuss?"

"*Señor* Garcia," Roha said. "Would it be possible to conduct our business in English?"

"I would be happy to discuss your project in English," he said in English.

Garcia crossed his legs. His body language was warm and relaxed, leaving Roha and Wyatt to assess if they were in the presence of a murderer and global criminal.

"Our project," Wyatt started. "First, you assure us this is confidential?"

"Of course."

Wyatt leaned forward.

"We're interested in adopting," he said. "We're researching adoptions."

"Adoptions?" Garcia's brow furrowed. "So." He took a moment. "You want to build an adoption center? Where will it be located?"

"No." Roha smiled and leaned forward. "We're researching the process of adopting a child."

"Adopting a child?" Garcia repeated, puzzled. "But why come to me, to us, here at Orchid Sea?"

"We understand," Wyatt said, "that you have knowledge about the process of international adoptions, and we're seeking your advice as a consultant because we're seriously considering it."

"We're willing to discuss your fees," Roha added.

"My fees?" Garcia looked at Wyatt, then Roha, then back to Wyatt. "I am sorry, but there's been a misunderstanding. Orchid Sea is an engineering consulting company. We consult on construction and building projects in Central and South America. We have nothing to do with adoptions. No, this is a mistake of some sort."

Roha and Wyatt sat back in silence.

Still puzzled, Garcia asked, "Are you police?"

Police?

At that moment, Wyatt's instincts—if he could trust them—told him that this man was not a fugitive, but a Honduran businessman.

"Police?" Wyatt repeated. "*Señor* Garcia, why would you ask us that?"

He looked at them, some of his warmth evaporating.

"Please, tell me who you are," Garcia said.

Wyatt and Roha exchanged a glance, with Roha nodding.

"*Señor* Garcia," Wyatt said, "we're journalists from the U.S., and we are researching adoptions. That's how your name came up."

"From who?"

"Our sources," Roha said.

"I don't understand. How could my name be linked to adoptions?"

"In our research, we learned that a man in Tegucigalpa, Honduras, named José Luís Garcia, an attorney, is knowledgeable about international adoptions."

"Attorney? But I'm not an attorney, and I know nothing of adoptions."

"Our apologies for this misunderstanding," Roha said.

For a moment, no one spoke.

"This is all quite strange," Garcia said. "First, police come to see me, and now two American journalists."

"Why did police visit you?" Wyatt asked. "Was it about adoptions?"

"No, they said nothing about that."

"What did they tell you?" Roha asked.

Garcia stared at them. "How can I be sure who you are?"

Roha and Wyatt showed him their identification, which seemed to assure Garcia.

"I don't know if I should tell you this."

"Sir, we will share with you anything we know."

"I am intrigued," Garcia said, then related what he knew.

"A few days ago, a Honduran detective and an FBI agent from the U.S. Embassy visited and asked me about my passport."

"What about it?" Roha said.

"It was lost, possibly stolen, a year ago while I was on a flight for business to Panama."

"What did the police ask you?"

"They wanted details as to how I lost it. Was it on the plane, or somewhere in transit? They wanted my airline, flight, hotel, that kind of thing. I gave them what I could."

"Did they tell you much more about their interest in your lost passport?"

Garcia shrugged.

"Not much. I told them that I feared identity theft, but nothing came of it."

"Really?" Roha said.

"I never had any issues. In all that time, I never had any indication that it was used wrongly. I never received any bills, inquiries, nothing."

"Did they tell you anything else?"

"They wanted to know if I had been to Los Angeles recently."

"Have you?"

"No. I have not been to the U.S. in years."

"Did they ask you anything more?"

"No, not—they were, as you say, tight-lipped. But wait, yes, they asked me about a man, although they never said why. They wanted to know if I received any mail, calls, any communication concerning a man, Ernesto something."

"Ernesto?" Wyatt said.

Garcia stood, went to his desk, opened a drawer and returned with a piece of paper. "I took it down. They wanted me to watch for anything, and call them if someone mentioned it. Here."

The name on the paper was Ernesto Ruiz Ayala.

"May we copy this?" Wyatt asked.

"I don't see why not," Garcia said.

Wyatt and Roha took it down, and then passed their numbers to Garcia.

"We apologize for the misunderstanding, *Señor* Garcia," Wyatt said. "Let's agree to keep each other posted on this, please."

"Yes, it's all very strange. So, it appears someone tied to adoptions, which must be criminal adoptions of some sort if police are involved, has used my passport. Very strange, indeed. And a little alarming."

Ernesto Ruiz Ayala.

It was the first time Roha and Wyatt had heard that name.

Stepping outside the building, they went to a bench where Roha made a call.

"I have a hunch," she told Wyatt.

Speaking into her phone, Roha launched into Spanish, saying the name Ernesto Ruiz Ayala, several times and slowly spelling it. A long moment passed, and she spoke again in short bursts, turned to Wyatt, and began nodding.

"Ayala is an attorney registered with the bar. He is with a firm in the city. The association will send us his bio."

CHAPTER 39

Guatemala City, Guatemala

The Deputy Commissioner's chair creaked as he leaned back, rocking and staring across his desk at Detective Sebastian Cruz.

Cruz was seated, with his boss to his left, and his partner, Detective Pablo Pineda, to his right.

Cruz could not see the Deputy Commissioner's eyes behind the tinted glasses he wore. Cruz thought the man's forearms were exceedingly hairy. Scowling, the Deputy Commissioner removed the unlit cigar from the corner of his mouth and placed it on an ashtray.

As the highest-ranking officer among them, he controlled their careers.

"I have read your preliminary report alleging an illegal adoption operation in Zone 15." The deputy tapped a hairy knuckle on Cruz's file folder on his desk. "Your request to investigate further is denied."

"Denied, sir?"

"Is your hearing impaired, Cruz?"

The deputy's chair creaked louder as he leaned forward.

"In your report, you say you were following a tip on gangs."

"Yes, sir."

"But this was not entirely true."

Cruz swallowed.

"You failed to state your true objective to your superior." The deputy nodded to Cruz's boss. "He was unable to inform me, in order to inform the people responsible for Zone 15. You misled your superiors. That's an insubordinate act."

Pineda's nerves got the better of him. He coughed, cleared his throat.

"And you state in your report," the deputy continued, "you took a car, which was sorely needed for other police business, and used it to observe the house for hours."

The deputy's breathing quickened; his nostrils flared as he continued.

"I called the commander for Zone 15, who informed me the house in question is a licensed childcare center for the children of ex pats, diplomats, and executives."

"We know it's licensed, but that could be a cover, sir, as I stated in my report."

The deputy's jaw tightened.

"Are you doubting the zone commander?"

"Sir, I —"

"What the hell's wrong with you, Cruz? Your job is working on gangs in your zone, not chasing some wild tip from this woman." He tapped the folder. "Are you fucking this housemaid, Cruz?"

"Sir?"

"Because this housemaid is screwing you."

"No, sir, it's not—"

"She's obviously trying to help her nephew by distracting you." The deputy then tapped his own head. "Use your brain, Cruz. Now get out."

Cruz's boss stopped them as they walked down the hall.

"You will both be penalized three days' pay."

Cruz nodded. Pineda clenched his fists.

"Get back to work. On gangs."

***

At their desks, Pineda cursed.

"I told you, Sebastian. Didn't I tell you this was idiotic?"

Deep in thought, Cruz didn't respond.

Pineda got up and stood over him.

"Are you not going to apologize?"

Cruz looked up at Pineda.

"No."

"No? You have dragged me into this. You have cost me pay. This will stain my record, hurt my chance for advancement."

"Pablo, think."

"Think? Think about what?"

Cruz gestured for Pineda to lean closer, and he lowered his voice.

"Something about this does not smell right. The brass was too quick and too forceful to dismiss this and steer us away. I know what I saw at that house, and it fits with the tip. Yes, I made mistakes. I should've done more checking before submitting my preliminary report."

"Let this go, Sebastian."

"Something's not right about this."

Pineda shook his head and threw up his hands, cursing under his breath.

"I'm talking to a wall. I need some air. I'm going outside. When I return, we'll work on gangs so we can get paid."

For several minutes, Cruz sorted files on his desk while thinking about the house in Zone 15. He didn't care about the reprimand, and he would endure the lost pay. He was convinced he had a lead to something significant. His phone rang.

"Hello, Detective. Karen Ceto, the public defender for Samuel Yaqui."

"Yes. Is your client prepared to cooperate and give us names?"

"No," Ceto said. "I'm calling for the status of your progress on the information Samuel's aunt provided you."

"Still under investigation."

"Well, we have something that may help." Cruz could hear the clicking of a keyboard. "I just sent you some photos."

Cruz's computer pinged with the notification of a new email with attached pictures. He began opening them.

"What are these?"

Ceto related how Cristina Yaqui's search for Quito the cat had led to her getting inside the walls of the alleged adoption house, where she took photos, five in all.

"Cristina seized on an opportunity," Ceto said. "It appears she's better at investigating than the PNC, which would make for an interesting story for the press, should this come to light in an unflattering way."

Ignoring the gibe, Cruz studied them—three of children and two of a white-haired man.

"How recent are these?" Cruz asked.

"Very recent. Taken yesterday."

"Does she know the identity of the man?"

"No."

"Are the people at the house aware she took these pictures?"

"No."

"What else did she say about them, about the residence?"

"She was there for a short time. The man at the gate said his name was Manny. She said there seemed to be a sense of tension and urgency."

"Urgency?"

"We don't know what that means, but we'll leave things with you. In the spirit of cooperation, we've provided you with significant information. We want Samuel released, and time is not our friend, Detective."

After the call, Cruz continued examining the photos, analyzing them within the context of what he knew about the house. The man on the phone seemed tense. *Why?* It seemed out of place for a childcare center. They were usually operated by women in a nurturing atmosphere. The white-haired man appeared to be under pressure.

Cruz was well aware the neighborhood was home to powerful people. *Who knows? Maybe they're being protected by members of the upper ranks?* There was precedent for bribes, payoffs, in exchange for protection.

He scrutinized the faces of the small children. Many appeared to be Guatemalan, but some were white. American? European? They could belong to diplomats or foreigners.

What if this is truly an illegal operation? Then where did these children come from? And what would happen to them if I walked away?

Anger bubbled in Cruz's gut.

He looked around his office, deciding to continue pursuing this but in secret. He tapped the keyboard of his computer for some numbers, and picked up his phone.

I should've gone deeper into this at the outset. I should have examined the license, rather than confirm the residence had one.

Cruz's first call was to the department of the Secretary of Social Welfare, to request copies of the license and permits for operating a childcare service inside the Zone 15 house. Then he called the Ministry of Public Health and Social Assistance for certificates for the property.

Next, he called the General Property Registry to learn who owned the house, and who was paying the property taxes.

Cruz was determined to find out if the house was a legitimate operation or not.

He went back to the two photos of the white-haired man.

Above all, he wanted to know who was operating it.

CHAPTER 40

Munich, Germany

"My name is Luca. I'm six…."

The boy smiled at Hanna Beck from the video on her phone.

Dressed in a plain white shirt, khaki pants, his hair combed neatly, Luca stood alone in a yard, a peach stucco wall and palm tree behind him.

"I like football. I like school. I like Dr. Seuss stories. *El Gato Ensombrerado* is my favorite," he said in English, then Spanish, to the camera. "I like pineapple, video games, and *Star Wars* movies."

Hanna and Deiter had just returned home from shopping. She'd purchased another book for the collection they were building. She couldn't resist sitting on the bed and playing Luca's recorded videos.

She'd lost count of how many times she'd watched them. Still, she fought tears when the camera pulled closer to Luca. The tiny scar on his temple was faded, but it evoked Luca's story.

His father and mother were missionaries from Canada, helping build schools and houses in remote regions. Two years ago, they were driving along a treacherous mountain road when their jeep rolled off the cliffside, crashed, and burned. Luca's parents were killed, but he survived.

No one in the missionary organization was in a position to take care of Luca on a long-term basis. Without any relatives in Canada, Luca's future became mired in bureaucracy between Guatemala and Canada. Learning of Luca's tragedy, an adoption agency, working with Guatemala's Child Protective Services, stepped forward to take Luca into its care.

That was Luca's case history, according to the adoption agency, which Deiter, through his contacts, had found online when they began their adoption journey.

It's how they found Luca.

At first Hanna had questions about the agency, about Luca being an orphaned foreign national and them being foreign nationals, and about complex adoption laws, but Deiter stopped her.

"Hanna, it's a special kind of agency," he said. "An agency that can make miracles happen. And a miracle is happening for us. Isn't Luca exactly the child we've been looking for?"

Yes, he is.

Hanna started another video of Luca, his face creased in concentration, answering questions about his young life.

"I remember some things about the fire....It was so hot....Someone was pulling me out...." Luca wiped at tears. "I miss my mom and my dad....I know I would be a good son for a new mom and dad...."

Hanna stopped the video.

It broke her heart, and she looked around the room they'd been preparing for Luca in their flat. The agency had informed them that they'd been approved, and all would be finalized and ready in three months. Dr. Seuss books, English and Spanish editions, were on the shelves, along with posters of *Star Wars* movies and Guatemala's national football team.

This is a good thing we're doing for an orphaned boy with no one in his life, she thought. Just as Gray, the doctor in Boston, told their support group about Timur in Afghanistan. It was no different for Luca.

He needs a family. He needs a chance at life.

In recalling the group, Hanna's thoughts shifted to Tamina and her pain. She wanted to send her another message, telling her to never give up. Miracles can happen.

Hanna adjusted her grip on her phone, when the sudden ringing of Deiter's phone echoed from the kitchen, where he was making a sandwich. Hanna halted and listened; he was talking to the agency.

Then Deiter called to her, and she joined him in the kitchen.

"Yes, Hanna's here with me."

Deiter placed his phone on the counter, and they leaned toward it.

"We've got you on speaker now. It's Isabel with the agency. Are you both there now?" Isabel said.

"Yes, we are." Hanna looked at Deiter.

"Good news. The process here has gone smoother than anticipated, enabling us to accelerate steps for you."

"What does that mean?" Hanna asked.

"The papers are ready now for you to sign and make the final deposit. We urge you to come as soon as you can. Luca's waiting for you to take him home."

"Really?" Hanna's hands were shaking.

"Yes, all is ready," Isabel said. "Keep me posted on your arrival. We'll go over some of the last details of the process when you get here."

"We will, Isabel," Deiter said. "Thank you."

"Yes, thank you for this wonderful news!" Hanna said.

After the call, Deiter and Hanna embraced.

"It's really happening," Deiter said, going to his desk and laptop. "We have a lot to do. We can't waste a moment."

They called their employers, to take the needed time off. Hanna, a former analyst with Germany's Federal Intelligence Service, the BND, now worked in corporate security. Deiter was an IT expert, who'd worked for

Germany's largest financial institutions. Since both had alerted their supervisors to their adoption situation, they were granted the needed time.

In between packing, Deiter checked flights.

"We can go direct on Lufthansa to Paris, Charles de Gaulle. Then Air France direct to Miami. Then direct from Miami on American."

"How soon?"

"We can leave tomorrow."

"Book us, Deiter."

CHAPTER 41

Paris, France

Early afternoon at Charles de Gaulle Airport.

Following their morning flight from Munich, and all security checks, Hanna and Deiter Beck, faces in their tablets, waited in preboarding at their gate for their Air France flight direct to Miami.

Deiter was double-checking their itinerary, tickets, and reservations. Arriving in Florida later that evening, they'd spend the night at the Sheraton. In the morning, they'd board their American flight direct to Tegucigalpa, Honduras.

Satisfied everything was good, Deiter went on to search other subjects, when Hanna turned to him.

"My God, Deiter, I can't believe how fortunate we are."

"Yes, we're fortunate." His eyes remained on his screen.

"Think of all the others in our support groups—those who've not been approved; those who've had the process stall, or change; and those who've been waiting, searching forever, like Tamina here in Paris."

"It's too bad that we don't have the time to actually meet her in person while we're here," Deiter said, continuing to work.

"I know. But I have an idea." Hanna repositioned her tablet and typed quickly for a few minutes before hitting send. "There, I've sent her a note, letting her know we're here at the airport. I've said that we're en route to get Luca, but thinking of her; that she mustn't give up believing a miracle will happen for her, too."

Deiter nodded his approval, and then tilted his screen. "Look," he said. "I've found more."

Even though their adoption groups protected identities by operating on a first-name basis, members had the option of privately messaging support to each other, if they chose to share an email address, which most did.

It enabled Deiter to apply his skills and, with help of some of Hanna's former intelligence colleagues, look deeper into the lives of support group members. They soon discovered that Tamina was a widowed billionaire heiress from Mykrekistan, who tried to keep a low profile while taking over for her ailing father—overseeing their global oil and gas operations, gold and diamond mines, and worldwide real estate properties.

The *Financial Times* reported Tamina's empire had recently acquired a conglomerate to manufacture electric trucks for the construction industry.

In addition to the building Tamina owned on the Champs-Élysées in Paris, she had a mansion overlooking Lake Geneva in Switzerland; a country estate in Surrey, England; a condo complex on Baker Street in London; a townhouse complex in Prague; a suite at the Plaza Hotel in New York City; a condo complex in Los Angeles; and villas in Spain and Italy.

But civil strife in Mykrekistan, and allegations linking her father to alleged corruption and bribery schemes, had Tamina living in exile while still grieving for her little boy, Rasul, and anticipating the death of her father.

Deiter pointed to an article and rare photo of Tamina in the *New York Times*, listing her as one of the world's richest women

Hanna nodded. The photo in the *Times* matched the face of the woman in their support group—Tamina, the art dealer in Paris.

"So much wealth, yet so much anguish for her," Hanna said.

Deiter agreed. "No matter how rich and powerful you are, you're not immune to the pain."

Hanna's tablet pinged, notifying her that she'd received a message—Tamina's response, which she read to Deiter.

"Thank you for your note, Hanna. My heart goes with you, Deiter, and Luca, along with my very best wishes for your new lives."

Deiter nodded, then showed Hanna a photo he'd found online of Tamina and Rasul on a tropical beach, the boy's eyes like stars as he laughs. Tamina's smile is radiant in the sun.

"Judging from the date, this was not long before his death," Deiter said.

"So, so sad," Hanna said, opening her latest photo of Luca. "Yes, we're blessed."

The speaker system near them came to life with the first boarding call for their flight to Miami.

CHAPTER 42

Tegucigalpa, Honduras

Ernesto Ruiz Ayala.

With his close-cropped, gray-white hair and strong facial features, Sabrena Roha considered Ayala handsome, smiling from her phone in the photo sent by the bar association.

Roha showed Ray Wyatt.

"This is our guy, Ray. I don't know the date of this photo, but he's a good-looking man."

Wyatt looked at Roha.

"Remember what Arthur Miller wrote in *The Crucible*, Sabrena. God thought Lucifer was beautiful in Heaven before he fell." He pointed to her phone. "Ayala could be a murdering monster; don't forget that."

"I know, Ray. Evil comes in all forms. I was just saying."

Roha closed the photo, and turned to the window of their taxi as it rolled along Boulevard Suyapa, the major avenue cutting across the city. Passing through the section where it divided Colonia Florencia north and south, she watched the buildings flow by.

They were heading for the law office the bar association gave for Ayala. Roha and Wyatt had reasoned that if Honduran police and an FBI agent from the U.S. Embassy had questioned José Luís Garcia about his missing passport; about recent trips to Los Angeles; and asked him about Ernesto Ruiz Ayala, who was listed as a lawyer registered with the bar association, then they had to be on the right track.

The taxi exited Boulevard Suyapa and traveled along a number of streets before coming to another professional building—this one, six stories of white stone and glass.

Standing on the sidewalk, Wyatt turned to Roha.

"I'm sorry. I was testy, Sabrena."

"Ray, forget it."

"It's just that I feel that somehow time's running out on us. And I still have trouble believing that the photo the FBI showed me is Danny. I want to believe it; that's why I'm here. But after all this time, I just—you know…"

"It's all right, Ray. It's okay. Let's keep working."

The office they wanted was on the fourth floor. They hadn't called ahead. Alone in the elevator, they agreed to, once again, proceed instinctively.

As the doors opened, they saw a sign with raised brass letters that said Sol Tierra & Marigold Law Firm.

They entered, and walked across the polished floors of the reception area to the dark wood desk of the receptionist.

"May I help you?" She gave them a warm smile.

"Yes." Roha presented a blank white business card, on which she'd neatly penned her name, Wyatt's name, her email, and phone number. "We're here to see Ernesto Ruiz Ayala."

"I'm sorry. That name again?"

Roha repeated: "Ernesto Ruiz Ayala."

The receptionist began shaking her head.

"No, I'm sorry, but no one by that name is with this office."

"But the Honduran Bar Association confirmed that he is with this firm."

"Excuse me." A woman in a tailored jacket and skirt emerged. "Who is it you're looking for?"

The receptionist's focus went from the woman, to Roha and Wyatt, then back to the woman, who projected authority.

"Ernesto Ruiz Ayala," Roha said.

"No, no, I'm sorry. No, no, there's no one here by that name," the woman said. "Perhaps someone else can help you? What is the nature of your business?"

"We're researching international adoptions and were hoping that—"

"Adoptions? No, I'm afraid we don't handle that. Our services encompass immigration, real estate, tax law, estate planning, but no, not adoptions."

"But the association said Mr. Ayala—"

Wyatt noticed the receptionist meekly studying Roha's card in her hand, as the woman, continuing to be icy, said, "I'm sorry, *señora* and *señor.*" The woman extended her arm politely toward the door. "But I'm afraid we cannot help you."

A moment later, Roha and Wyatt were back in the elevator, and then on the street.

"That was weird," Wyatt said.

"You got most of that?"

"Pieces, but the woman's tone, her body language and the way the receptionist eyeballed the exchange…"

"Something's up," Roha said.

"Let's take a walk around the block," Wyatt said. "I'm thinking of something we can try."

Halfway around the block, Roha's phone rang. The number was blocked. She answered, glancing at the building as she spoke in Spanish. It was the receptionist at the law firm.

"You look like nice people who want to adopt?" The receptionist was almost whispering.

"Yes, we're looking into it. Can you help us?"

"No, but I thought my boss was rude. They're all scared here."

"Why?"

"Ernesto Ruiz Ayala used to be with the firm, but they fired him quite a while ago. I never knew why. But police were here asking about him only a few days ago."

"Really? Why?"

"I don't know, it was all hush-hush. And the lawyers here don't want to have anything to do with him. Don't want to admit he worked here. I think you scared them."

"Scared them?"

"Something's wrong, and I just think nice people like you should know this before you go looking for Ayala. Be very careful."

"That's so helpful. Do you know how we can find him?"

"No."

CHAPTER 43

Tegucigalpa, Honduras

Later that day, Roha and Wyatt were in Barrio San Rafael.

Their taxi had dropped them in a narrow, curving, hilly section of two-story and three-story pastel buildings. Parked cars lined both sides of the street. Leafy trees leaned over walls and gated yards, creating pools of shade.

Roha and Wyatt had made a number of checks online, and then several calls before deciding to come here to *Diaz Hermanas Investigación Privada,* according to the sign posted at the steel-gated entrance of the two-story, mint-colored stucco building.

Roha pushed the button and announced their arrival into the intercom. A woman's voice invited them to the second floor. The lock buzzed, then clicked open; they entered.

After striking out at the law firm in their search for Ernesto Ruiz Ayala, they checked his name with their sources in the U.S. Roha had reached out to the flight attendants, hoping they could ask the detective in Mexico who was on the Stroud investigation.

Wyatt had called his friend, DeCastilla, the retired NYPD detective. But Wyatt held off calling Jill McDade at the FBI, because he didn't want her knowing he was in Central America trying to find Danny.

Roha and Wyatt's efforts stalled. None of the people they had contacted knew Ayala's name. Their sources had promised to keep checking and get back as soon as they had something.

"We could be spinning our wheels, waiting for days, Sabrena," Wyatt said, suggesting they hire a private investigator to help them.

Roha agreed.

They called several agencies, stating how they needed to locate Ayala. Most of the big agencies were uninterested, saying they were busy, advising that it would take a week, or longer, before they could help. Wyatt then suggested that when calling the next agency, Roha say, "I'll pay five hundred U.S. cash today, if you can get me an up-to-date address for a person we need to locate."

The Diaz agency accepted, inviting them to its office right away.

Now, Roha and Wyatt headed upstairs to the agency's office. It was one large room, plain and tasteful, with hardwood floors, a ceiling fan, and outswing doors that opened wide, capturing breezes from the canopied balcony.

A woman rose from her desk to greet them. She was in her 40s, hair pulled into a ponytail, and wearing a red print shirt and jeans.

"Gabriela Diaz," she said, smiling, shaking their hands, and then indicating the chairs before her desk.

"Could you give me a little background. All information will help me help you," Diaz said, sitting at her desk, taking a pencil and pad next to her laptop.

Roha outlined that they were journalists investigating an illegal adoption ring and looking to locate Ernesto Ruiz Ayala, a Honduran attorney. She showed her Ayala's photo from the bar association. Then, as Diaz requested, Roha and Wyatt produced their IDs.

"American journalists," Diaz said, studying their press IDs. Roha spelled out Ayala's full name for her. "One moment."

Diaz began typing on the keyboard of her laptop, searching. Wyatt figured she was checking for True Signal News stories, bylines and staff bios, to support their IDs. The fan blades above her rotated slowly. Eventually, Diaz took one of the four phones on her desk and made a call.

She launched into Spanish, talking softly, smiling, joking, then saying and spelling Ayala's full name. After that, she made other chatty calls, as if gossiping with friends. She used different phones for the calls. Ending the last one, she smiled at Roha and Wyatt.

"Now, we wait. It shouldn't be long."

"Let us pay you," Roha said, counting out $250. "As discussed, half now and half with an address."

Diaz put the cash in an envelope, then locked it in her desk. "Do you require a receipt?"

"We'll get it when we're done," Roha said. "Can we continue in English, for my colleague's benefit?"

"Forgive me, my English is not so good, but I'll try."

"What is your background?" Wyatt asked.

"I was a police officer for ten years. Then ten years ago, I quit after my sister was murdered. She was a journalist doing a story on gangs and corruption."

"We're sorry to hear that," Roha said.

"The agency is called the Diaz Sisters, to honor her."

"It's a beautiful thing to do. Is that her with you?"

Roha nodded to a framed photo on the desk of Diaz and a woman, both smiling.

"Yes, that is Maria."

"I am curious. Who did you call just now?" Wyatt asked.

"I called a friend in Transportation, to search for Ayala's license and photo, to match what you have. I also have a friend who works with our national ID cards. I also called friends with records in utilities and electricity, and telecommunications. To see if he is listed on any bills."

"And you work alone?"

"Yes, a small, low-profile operation. I call on contractors if I need them. I recently closed a case for the attorney of a tourist, assaulted by a staff member at a luxury hotel. They made a big payout to halt a lawsuit and prevent bad press. I was paid well for my work, because it made the case. Can I get you a coffee, a soft drink?"

The reporters declined. While waiting, they heard the echo of a rooster's crow. Wyatt watched bedsheets on a clothesline, waving in a breeze in a neighboring yard below.

"Why so many phones?" Wyatt asked.

"Burners to protect my sources. I get new ones every few weeks."

A notification sounded on Diaz's laptop as one of her phones rang. Typing and talking, she turned the screen to show a driver's license with Ayala's photo.

Roha and Wyatt were encouraged, but saw no address.

"Addresses are not required to be listed on a Honduran license," Diaz said after the call. "Do not worry. I'll have something shortly."

Another phone rang, with Diaz taking notes during a short conversation.

"Good." Diaz ended the call. "We have an address. We'll take my car."

***

Diaz's white Honda CRV had the pleasant smell of a new car.

Leaving her neighborhood, they traveled a short stretch on the expressway before she exited, navigating nearer to their destination.

"It's coming up," Diaz said, turning her head to the commercial buildings along Boulevard la Hacienda, not far from the university.

Roha and Wyatt studied the supermarket, car rental agency, health clinic, and other businesses.

"There," Diaz said. "It's in there." She'd nodded to a commercial plaza with a pharmacy, a food take-out outlet, a dentist, and then an office, with a sign reading something about *Servicio De Ma*—. Wyatt missed it as they went by. "I'll park down a bit, out of sight," Diaz said.

After turning into the parking lot of a large mall, she shut the motor off.

"I wanted to see it first," Diaz said. "It's *Servicio De Manera Clara*, which sort of means, service for a clear way. They offer private legal assistance for asylum seekers, refugees, and foreign nationals—and adoptions. It would be a perfect front for an illegal adoption network."

"And how is Ayala connected to this?" Wyatt looked back at the plaza.

"His name is on the utility bills for the office."

"But it doesn't look like a facility to keep children," Roha said, looking at the building.

"Could be the administrative arm," Diaz said. "Wait here. I'll check it out."

They watched her walk to the plaza, try the door. It was locked. A moment passed. The door cracked open, a woman appeared, and Diaz spoke briefly with her. Diaz nodded her thanks, then went to the take-out food outlet. A few minutes later, she returned with a food order.

"Okay, that's the place. I didn't see Ayala. It's closed today, but will open tomorrow morning. I'll give you some suggestions on how to approach them when you go back tomorrow. On a hunch, I went to the take-out place, showed them Ayala's photo. I said I was looking for a long-lost uncle, who may work in the area and doesn't know his estranged mother is dying." Diaz sorted the contents of the take-out bag. "Sure enough, they recognized Ayala as a customer. So, there you go. Would you like a *baleada*?"

CHAPTER 44

Guatemala City, Guatemala

Amid the traffic, the music, and aromas of the markets near the plaza in Zone 1, Detective Sebastian Cruz studied the handicrafts displayed on the vendors' tables.

But his thoughts drifted.

More than a day had passed since he'd secretly sought records for the childcare service operating in the Zone 15 house. He was growing nervous, still waiting for a response.

In the wake of the reprimand, Cruz had assured his partner, Pablo Pineda, that he would only work on gangs. But it was not true.

Cruz had refused to give up. Something about what he'd seen that day at the house; and something about Cristina Yaqui's tip; and something about the way the brass dismissed it, told him to keep investigating.

Secretly.

Yes, even if it costs me my job.

He took out his phone, and again, looked at Cristina Yaqui's photos that the lawyer, Ceto, had sent. He looked at the children—children who were possibly victims of illegal adoption.

I can't walk away from this and live with myself.

Cruz had told Pineda he was meeting a gang source in the market. Cruz was also shopping for his daughter's birthday gift, going from table to table; he grew anxious because his request for records was taking so long.

Too long.

There could be many reasons for delays. It was true that nearly all of the government's records had been computerized years ago. But systems crashed, workloads got backlogged. Maybe someone had informed the brass of his requests, Cruz thought. What if the address had been flagged?

If he lost his job, he'd contact his cousin about a position in private security for the resort hotels in Antigua, and move his family there.

"The finest quality, *señor*." The vendor nodded to the worry dolls Cruz was considering. "They're handmade by my grandmother in her village."

The five tiny dolls, each no bigger than a coffee bean, were dressed in traditional Mayan style. The dolls would take on your worries if you placed them under your pillow at night, according to legend. These were the kind his daughter had wanted, Cruz's wife had told him. They came in a colorful, handwoven cotton bag.

"I'll take them," Cruz said, paying and thinking that he should also get some worry dolls for himself.

His phone rang. It was a clerk from the General Property Registry.

"I have the information you requested."

Cruz listened, then hurried back to his office, the worry dolls tucked safely in his pocket.

***

Pablo Pineda was there at his desk when Cruz returned to his.

"Hey, Sebastian, how did it go with your gang source?"

"Not good, Pablo. He stood me up."

Pineda eyed his partner a moment longer than necessary, leaving the tension in the air as he got up and stood over him.

"You know," Pineda said. "I was thinking we should take another run at that kid, Samuel Yaqui. See if he's reconsidered giving up names."

"It's worth a shot. His court date's been pushed back," Cruz said.

"Right. I'm going to get something to eat, while I can still afford it."

"Very funny."

"You want to come?"

"No, I have work."

"Want me to bring you anything?"

"No thanks, Pablo."

Pineda looked at him and nodded.

Checking to ensure he was alone in their area, Cruz opened his email from the clerk at the General Property Registry. It came with a summary of the records, showing who owned the house in Zone 15.

It was registered to a company.

Manera Clara.

Records showed the principal officers of *Manera Clara* were Emma Vallejo and Ernesto Ruiz Ayala.

The names meant nothing to Cruz. He was considering his next steps when he received a new email, this one in response to his checking with Social Welfare, requesting copies of the license and permits for operating a childcare service at the house. It appeared to be a legitimate licensed childcare service. Again, the same company name and the same officers: Emma Vallejo and Ernesto Ruiz Ayala.

Nothing out of the ordinary there.

Cruz decided to run the names through Guatemala's national police databases. He had access to them, and it would take only a few minutes. Typing, watching, and searching, Cruz found nothing for a complaint, arrest, or criminal history for either Vallejo or Ayala.

Sticking out his lower lip, he thought.

Maybe there is truly nothing to this. He could abandon it, with no harm done. But those photos, what he saw himself at the house, and the account Cristina Yaqui had given him, echoed until the obvious struck him.

Of course! If this was allegedly a global operation, he needed to check that international connection with the national Criminal Investigations Department. Fortunately, Cruz had a good friend—Fernando, a boyhood pal he trusted with his life—who worked in the department's National Central Bureau, with the unit handling investigations that have global tentacles.

Cruz reached into his desk for a hard-to-trace burner phone he used.

He would get Fernando to check the names with police forces in other countries, and run them through Interpol. For good measure, he sent along a photo of the mystery man Cristina Yaqui had photographed at the house, the man with the neat white hair.

Let's see where that leads.

CHAPTER 45

Tegucigalpa, Honduras

The next morning, Roha and Wyatt were seated in the waiting area of *Servicio De Manera Clara*, a clipboard on Roha's lap, completing forms for the agency's adoption services.

The evening before, they had taken Gabriela Diaz to dinner where they paid her the balance and discussed their situation.

They knew that international adoptions had many restrictions, but were legal in Honduras, unlike neighboring Guatemala. For years, Guatemala had halted adoptions by foreigners to thwart abuses such as corruption and exploitation involving abductions, and the trafficking and sale of children.

"But with the limitations imposed by Honduras," Diaz had said, "and the demand likely exceeding the supply, it may be tempting for criminals here to look to Guatemala, with its population nearly double that of Honduras, as a source of children."

"Do you have any thoughts on our approach?" Roha said.

"I think," Diaz said, "as you've indicated, be flexible as the situation demands. Go there, start the process, maybe drop Ernesto Ayala's name. Try to get a location of where the agency's children are."

Roha and Wyatt nodded.

"But always keep in your head," Diaz said, "that this Ayala, this man, is a dangerous murder suspect. You must be ready for anything."

At that, Roha had closed her eyes briefly, seeing the rat hole in San Pedro at the Port of Los Angeles where Wanda Stroud's corpse was found. And Wyatt recalled the hotel fire where he had lost Danny.

"We know," Wyatt said.

So now here they were, in the office of *Servicio De Manera Clara*, completing preliminary paperwork. When they'd finished, Roha gave it to the assistant behind the plastic shield of the reception desk.

The nerves in Wyatt's chest tightened.

Was he really closer to Danny? Or was this all part of his never-ending nightmare?

He took in the banality of the room. It was much like any waiting room in a suburban dentist or doctor's office—plain furniture, an assortment of outdated magazines, cheap art on the wall.

An air conditioner rattled and hummed.

Was this the gateway to the illegal adoption network that had Danny?

No sign of Ayala, so far.

Across from them, a bearded man, his long blondish hair tied in a man bun, worked with a woman, with brown hair and bangs, next to him to complete forms on a clipboard. Beside them, another couple—the man, with short-cropped hair and a white T-shirt with a small Union Jack; the woman, in a ponytail and printed top—had their faces in their phones. They glanced up when an office door opened, and a woman said, "*Señor* and *Señora* Helliwell?"

The Union Jack and ponytail couple pocketed their phones and stood. As they entered, Wyatt heard the office woman say, "I'm Martina. Welcome...."

At that moment, another couple entered from outside. The woman had short blond hair and wore a powder-blue top. The man had a navy polo shirt, which accentuated his neat blond hair.

Wyatt put them in their early 40s.

They went to the receptionist, with the blue-top woman stating: "Hanna and Deiter Beck, to see Isabel."

The receptionist told them to wait. The Becks sat next to Roha and Wyatt, nodding with polite smiles.

The bun-and-bangs couple looked up from their clipboard, observing the comings and goings. Hanna Beck searched her bag, while Deiter Beck sat back, extended his legs, and dragged his hands over his face.

Picking up on the couple's casualness, Roha took a chance.

"Hi." She smiled. "We're Sabrena and Ray from the U.S."

Hanna exchanged a quick glance with Deiter, who shrugged.

"Hanna and Deiter from Germany," Hanna said, in English with a mild accent.

"Are you here for an adoption?" Roha asked.

The Becks exchanged another quick look.

"Yes," Hanna said. "And you?"

"We're at the very beginning. How about you?"

"We're at the final stage," Hanna said with a smile. "We're picking up our son."

"Oh my God!" Roha put her hands on her heart. "That's wonderful."

"Are you getting him here?" Wyatt asked.

"Not here." Deiter sat up, put his elbows on his knees. "Here, we sign final papers, make payments. Then they'll instruct us on collecting Luca."

"Luca?" Sabrena said. "That's a nice name."

"Yes. He's six," Hanna said.

"Do you have a picture?" Roha asked. "Could we see him?"

Turning to Deiter, who nodded, Hanna produced her phone and swiped through several photos of Luca for Roha and Wyatt.

As Roha cooed with Hanna, Wyatt stared at the images.

He caught his breath.

He kept staring, blood thumping in his ears, his scalp prickling as the world stopped turning. Wyatt was transfixed by the boy's eyes, his mouth, and his face. Each cued photo of this six-year-old boy was a spike piercing his heart.

This can't be.

But it was true.

This boy is my son.

This boy is Danny.

Wyatt's pulse kicked up, and he turned to feign a cough, disguising his reaction to the photo. Turning back, he looked at Hanna and Deiter.

"What do you know about Luca's history?" Wyatt asked.

Hanna blinked several times.

"His parents were missionaries," Hanna said. "They were killed when their car crashed a couple of years ago, and—"

"*Señor* Wyatt and *Señora* Roha?" a woman reading from a clipboard said from the open office door.

Roha stood, while Wyatt regained his composure and joined her.

"Good luck," Hanna whispered to them, putting her phone away.

***

The woman seated Roha and Wyatt across from her desk.

She wore a skirt and an aqua-green blazer jacket. She had strawberry blond hair. Her face was mapped with freckles.

"Welcome. My name is Isabel. Would you prefer to continue in Spanish or English?" she said in Spanish, then repeated in English.

"English, please." Wyatt cleared his throat, grappling with the reality that a few feet away, Hanna and Deiter Beck from Germany were about to adopt his son.

So close. I'm so close to Danny.

Wyatt battled to remain calm and find some way of alerting Roha.

She'd taken a tissue from her bag, was twisting it in her hands.

"Very well." Isabel smiled. "I see, Ray, you work in New York, and Sabrena, in California. And you're not married."

"We'll be married in a few months," Roha said. "We wanted to start the adoption process because it takes so long."

Nodding, Isabel placed her palms flat on the clipboard holding their completed forms.

"I must apologize. I realize you've traveled so far. But the truth is, you do not meet our requirement: You must be married for at least two years."

"We understand," Roha said, "but many agencies allow a single woman to adopt."

"Yes, but we are unlike other agencies. Perhaps you could reapply in two years, and bring your marriage certificate?"

"Two years? No!" Roha said.

"I'm sorry, Sabrena."

"You don't understand, Isabel," Roha said. "We've tried so many other agencies. I can't have children, and in vitro is not an option. You are our only hope, now. Won't you please help us?"

Roha twisted the tissue as Isabel paged through the forms.

"I see you left the referral blank," she said. "Who referred you? How did you know about us?"

"We learned about you online," Roha said.

"Online?"

Sensing this chance to get closer to Danny was slipping away, Wyatt said, "It is our understanding that *Señor* Ayala would help us."

Isabel looked at him, her warmth cooling.

"And how do you know him?"

"Our friends online," Wyatt said.

Isabel nodded, and went back to the forms.

"You list your profession as writers. Are you journalists?"

"No, not really," Wyatt said.

"Who do you write for? What do you write?"

"Travel and food stories," Wyatt said. "For airline magazines, that sort of thing. We're more freelance travel writers."

"And you are from Los Angeles and New York City?"

"Yes," Roha said. "It's on the forms. We plan to marry, adopt, and have a family. There must be something you can do to help us."

Isabel stood, taking the clipboard.

"Please wait here."

She left the room. The moment the door closed, Wyatt seized Roha's wrist, and urgently whispered, "That boy the Germans are adopting is Danny!"

Roha's jaw dropped. "Are you certain?"

"I swear to you, it's the same boy McDade and the FBI identified with age progression. It's Danny."

"My God, Ray."

"We're so close."

"I'll keep pleading with Isabel."

"She's suspicious about us. She's likely making calls, checking bylines. Meanwhile, we could lose Hanna and Deiter." Wyatt surveyed Isabel's desk for anything to indicate where the children were kept. He spotted a file folder labeled BECK.

It could have information on Danny's location.

Wyatt's mind raced. He considered taking it. Then he thought of opening it, photographing pages. He reached for it, when the doorknob turned. Leaving the file untouched, he sat back and put his arm around Roha.

Isabel returned, holding the clipboard to her chest, and remained standing at her desk.

"I had a quick call with my director. We'd like to place you on a waiting list. We have your information, and we'll alert you to an opening."

"That's it?" Roha's voice broke.

"I'm sorry, Sabrena. I'm sorry, Ray," Isabel said. "Now, if you'll excuse me, I have an appointment."

"Isabel, please, I beg you to help us."

Isabel stood next to her open door.

"Have a safe trip back to the U.S."

Roha and Wyatt stood. Wyatt glanced back at the Beck file.

Is it my last link to Danny?

CHAPTER 46

Guatemala City, Guatemala

At his home, Detective Sebastian Cruz watched the little girls giggling in their party dresses as Elina, his daughter, opened her birthday gifts.

"A puzzle game!" she said, unwrapping the last one, smiling. But Cruz detected a hint of disappointment and winked at his wife.

"Oh, Elina," his wife teased. "I think there's one last gift."

Elina looked around the room. So did her friends.

"Where?"

"Under your chair," Cruz said.

Finding it, Elina tore open the wrapping, discovering the worry dolls.

"Oh, thank you! Thank you!"

Cruz basked in Elina's laughter and his wife's approving smile just as his burner phone rang. Stepping away from the party, he answered. It was Fernando at the National Central Bureau.

"Sebastian, I got a hit from Interpol on the name you gave me."

"Ayala?"

"Yes, Ernesto Ruiz Ayala. He's a big deal. Interpol has a Red Notice for him; wanted by the U.S. for a murder in

Los Angeles, suspected human trafficking, and several other crimes. The photo in Interpol's Red Notice fits with the one you sent me."

Cruz went into his bedroom and shut the door, his thoughts blazing.

"Fernando, who else have you alerted to this?"

"No one else—yet. Just you. But a Red Notice means our unit must arrest Ayala as soon as possible. I must alert my supervisor, who'll advise your boss and the people in Zone 15, so we can plan an operation."

"No, Fernando! Hold on! Listen, it's critical that this goes down the right way. Ayala may have bought protection. Do you understand?"

Fernando said nothing.

"We can't risk this getting out to the wrong people," Cruz said. "Do you understand?"

Fernando absorbed the significance in silence.

"Do you understand, Fernando? This information never came from me. My boss and the people in Zone 15 cannot know what we know."

"Yes, Sebastian, but I am required to report the origin of the information for the judge to issue an arrest warrant. You know that's how it is."

"Listen, the tip—my tip to you—will *officially* come very soon, but from the Americans. It will go to the ministry, then down through the chain."

"But these things take time, and that could delay it longer."

"Not so much. The Americans will want to get this moving. So, you do nothing but wait. If anyone notices your Interpol query, say you are still confirming your information. Just delay. I assure you the order will thunder down from the top of the chain. Can you do this, Fernando?"

"Yes, but you make me very nervous, Sebastian."

After his call, Cruz opened his wallet, and plucked out a business card for Tom Fletcher, the FBI's legal attaché at the U.S. Embassy in Guatemala City. Cruz had met Fletcher at joint intel-sharing sessions about gangs.

Turning the card over, he saw the number Fletcher had penned for his secure phone, and called it.

It took four rings before Fletcher answered.

It took 10 minutes for Cruz to tell him that Ayala, the suspect the U.S. wanted for a murder in Los Angeles and other global crimes, was operating an illegal adoption ring in Zone 15. Cruz stressed the sensitivity to Fletcher, guiding him on how the U.S. should make a request through the ministry to initiate the procedure for a warrant, so NCB could arrest Ayala, rescue children, and start extradition proceedings.

"Leave it with us," Fletcher said. "Sebastian, thanks for this."

Sitting on his bed, Cruz reviewed everything in his head.

It would take a day, maybe more, to assemble the paperwork before the judge would issue the warrant, and the NCB could launch an operation at the house in Zone 15. But Cruz had set it all in motion. In fact, the maid, Cristina Yaqui, had set it all in motion. Cruz could only pray that everything went according to plan.

His job was on the line.

Taking a breath, he returned to his daughter's party. His wife, serving cake to the girls, looked at him.

"Everything okay, Sebastian?"

"Yes. Everything's okay."

Cruz smiled at Elina's worry dolls, which were next to her on the table.

CHAPTER 47

Tegucigalpa, Honduras

Stepping from Isabel's office, Roha tried to stifle her sobbing.

Wyatt took her shoulders, comforting her as they walked through the waiting area. Hanna and Deiter looked at them with concern just as Isabel, standing at her door, called the Becks.

Ignoring the call, Hanna touched Roha's arm.

"What's happened, Sabrena?" Hanna asked.

Hands still on her face, Roha shook her head, leaving it for Wyatt to answer. "We were rejected."

"Oh no," Hanna said.

Watching them, Isabel repeated, "Hanna and Deiter Beck."

"We're so sorry." Deiter patted Wyatt's shoulder.

Nodding his appreciation, Wyatt pulled Roha closer to him, and they continued to the door.

Outside, they went to a bench in the shade near the office's storefront.

"We can't lose the German couple," Wyatt said, tapping Roha's knee. "You were good in there, Sabrena."

Nodding, Roha collected herself.

"Here's what we'll do," Wyatt said. "I'll go behind the plaza to watch the back. You stay here, watch the front. We'll text when we see them leave."

Roha nodded. "How do we play it?"

"We're devastated. We'll ask for their advice," Wyatt said. "We have to find out where they're going to get Danny."

"All right."

"Sabrena, this may be the only chance we get."

Roha nodded. Wyatt made his way to the back of the plaza.

Twenty minutes later, the sun flashed on the door of *Servicio De Manera Clara*. Hanna and Deiter stepped out, and Roha texted Wyatt.

"Front!"

Seeing Roha, Hanna sat with her, placing her hand on her knee.

"We're so sorry for what happened, Sabrena," Hanna said.

Feigning tears, Roha nodded.

"We've been turned down by so many agencies. We'd heard such good things about *Servicio De Manera Clara*. We were so hopeful. We even believed they'd introduce us to some of the children."

Hanna and Deiter were silent.

"I'm sorry for the waterworks display," Roha said.

"Don't be. This is hard," Hanna said.

"It was painful for me in there," Roha said. "We need to pull ourselves together."

"Where's Ray?" Deiter asked.

Roha turned toward to the take-out food outlet to see Wyatt round the corner.

"There he is," Roha said.

Wyatt joined them.

"We're so sorry for you," Hanna said.

"Very unfair," Deiter said.

"Thank you. I guess you've been through the ups and downs."

"Oh, yes," Deiter said, nodding.

"And now you're here to get your child," Wyatt said. "You must be thrilled."

"We are," Hanna said.

"Where are you picking him up?" Roha asked.

Hanna and Deiter traded a quick look with each other.

"Sorry," Roha touched a tissue to her eyes. "None of my business."

"Oh, no," Hanna said. "They're sending us information on that. We just did the final paperwork and paid the last fees."

"Excuse us. We need to get back to our hotel and get ready." Deiter looked to the street as a taxi wheeled into the lot. "I think that's for us. Good luck to you."

"Yes." Hanna smiled, touching Roha's hand. "Never give up hope."

"Wait," Wyatt said. "Maybe we can share the taxi? What hotel are you staying in?"

More uneasy glances passed between Hanna and Deiter.

"We're at the Intercontinental," Hanna said, turning back to Deiter. "But really, I don't think—"

"We're at the Marriott," Wyatt said. "It's nearby. We can drop you off. It's on us."

Deiter looked at the taxi stopping near them.

"Thank you, but we really don't think—"

"Please. We could use your advice on the process," Wyatt said.

"Especially from people who've succeeded." Roha blinked back tears. "Especially now."

Hanna looked at Deiter; her eyes softened into surrender.

"All right," Deiter said.

CHAPTER 48

Tegucigalpa, Honduras

Their taxi was a Toyota Corolla.

Wyatt took the front seat next to the driver; Roha and the Becks were in the back. They pulled away, and the city flowed by.

"Tell us, Ray, where in America are you from?" Deiter asked.

"I'm based in New York. Sabrena's in L.A."

"And what do you do?" Hanna asked.

"We're both writers, for magazines, online sites," Roha said. "And you?"

"Our home is Munich," Deiter said. "Hanna is with corporate security, and I'm with IT."

"And no biological children?" Roha asked.

"No, not for us. And you?"

"The same," Roha said. "How long was the process for you to get to this stage?"

"About a year," Hanna said. "We just keep at it."

Aware the drive to the hotel was short, Wyatt had an idea.

"Hanna," he turned from his seat. "Would you allow us to see your photos of Luca again?"

Hanna pulled her phone from her bag, cued up the photos, passed her phone to Roha, who swiped and cooed. "There's a video of him that I love." Hanna pointed.

"Luca's such a sweet-looking boy," Roha said after she finished viewing, then passed Hanna's phone to Wyatt. "Isn't he sweet, Ray?"

Turning in his seat, lowering Hanna's phone to his lap, Wyatt silenced his click-sound feature on his phone as he secretly recorded the photos and the video, his brain and heart thundering.

This is Danny. This is my son.

In one close-up photo, Wyatt noticed a scar on the boy's temple.

Is that from the hotel fire?

Wyatt ached to reach into the phone and pull Danny from it, to bring him home. But he concentrated, working fast, while Roha continued talking to the Becks. He swiped deeper into Hanna's photos in a futile effort to find a hint of where they might be headed. Instead, he found selfies of Hanna and Deiter, copied them, then turned and returned the phone.

"He's a good-looking boy," Wyatt said. "Deiter, tell me again about his history. You were saying his parents were killed."

"We were told they were missionaries from Canada, working deep in the country. A couple years ago, their car crashed off a mountain road and burned. They were killed, but Luca survived. But there were bureaucratic complications returning him to Canada. He had no other family, so the agency arranged to take him and, well, here we are."

"Poor Luca. That's so tragic," Roha said.

"It tore me to pieces," Hanna said.

"Help me understand the process," Wyatt said. "You're German. Luca's Canadian, or Honduran. So how do you leave the country, and then enter Germany with him? I mean, how does it all work—passport, documentation—immigration-wise?"

"The agency takes care of all of that," Deiter said. "That's why they're so exclusive, and so expensive. Their skill is streamlining the process. I expect our exit with Luca will not be entirely traditional."

"What do you mean?" Wyatt said.

"You know about Ernesto?"

Wyatt glanced at Roha, who gave a little nod, and then said: "Do you mean Ernesto Ayala?"

Hanna nodded.

Wyatt glanced at Roha again, indicating a confirmation.

"No. I mean, we've heard his name," Wyatt said.

"Perhaps it's early in the process for you." Deiter looked out to the buildings. "When you get further along and meet him and Emma, you'll know more about their connections and how the agency operates."

"I hope we make it that far," Wyatt said.

"You both got this far, through your channels," Hanna said. "Getting to this stage is a sign that you're in. It just takes a little time."

"And a lot of money, as I'm sure you already know," Deiter said. "Here we are."

The taxi stopped at the Diamond Sky Plaza, and the Becks got out.

"Hold it." Wyatt and Roha got out with them, but the taxi waited. "You've been so helpful. Please, let us buy you lunch, or drinks?"

"That's very kind, but not necessary," Hanna said.

Deiter shook Wyatt's hand.

"Have a safe trip back to America, Ray, and don't give up hope."

"Thank you for your help and your understanding," Roha said, hugging Hanna. "Good luck with Luca."

"Don't be discouraged, Sabrena," Hanna said. "Be persistent with the agency, and it will happen for you."

After watching the Becks enter the hotel, Wyatt and Roha had their taxi take them a block away. They got out, paid the driver, and then hurried back to the Diamond Sky Plaza.

Roha went to the front desk. She confirmed that the Becks were registered as guests and got their room number. Then she joined Wyatt, sitting on a sofa in a far corner of the lobby behind potted palms, offering cover but with a view to the hotel's main doors.

Wyatt's heart raced as he swiped through the photos of Danny he'd copied from Hanna Beck's phone. Staring at them he saw his son at six, recognizing Lisa's features in Danny's face. Watching the video, hearing Danny's voice, Wyatt's eyes filled with tears.

"We can't lose them, Sabrena. They're our only lead to Danny. We'll do whatever it takes. We cannot lose them."

Keeping her eyes on the desk and the hotel doors, Roha had taken up her phone. "We're not going to lose them, Ray."

"Who're you calling?"

"Gabriela Diaz. We need all the help we can get."

A moment later, Roha, speaking quickly in Spanish, told Diaz everything. After the call, she turned to Wyatt.

"She'll help us. She said to sit tight right here."

"We're not moving."

As time passed, Wyatt assessed their surroundings.

"Sabrena, this place must have several exits that we can't cover."

"I know, but if they check out or get a taxi, the front's our best bet."

Pulse pounding, Wyatt ran through scenarios and options, deciding to text his friend Tony DeCastilla, to see if he'd learned anything further on Ernesto Ruiz Ayala. While waiting, Wyatt, now verging on desperation, considered calling Jill McDade at the FBI, but dismissed the idea. As he waited, his phone vibrated with DeCastilla's response.

"You could be onto something. Let me keep working on it, Ray."

Wyatt texted: "Tony, need an address for Ayala ASAP."

DeCastilla responded: "Hang tough, buddy."

Twenty minutes went by when Roha's phone rang.

She spoke in Spanish, mouthing to Wyatt that it was Diaz. After a short conversation, she relayed the information to him.

"Ray, the Becks used the hotel's service to book two airline tickets on a flight to Guatemala City tomorrow."

CHAPTER 49

Los Angeles, California

Francisco Sousa's eyes shone, like falling stars.

Such a sweet-looking boy, Special Agent Jill McDade thought.

Francisco was three when he disappeared while with his family at a mall in São Paulo, Brazil. Next on the screen: Becky Layne, aged two, when she went missing from a grocery store parking lot in San Antonio, Texas. Next: Martin Wakeman, aged four, disappeared while with his family near the London Eye. Next: Sophie Hernandez, three, when she vanished while with her father on the Madrid Metro. Then Danny Wyatt, vanished in a hotel fire while on vacation with his family in Banff, Canada.

Ray's son.

Five angelic faces.

Variations—all age-progressed—staring back at McDade from her screen.

Then Wanda Stroud's warm, friendly face appeared—a widowed, retired librarian, loved by everyone who knew her.

And here is her killer.

McDade clicked to the handsome, white-haired man in his 50s. His alias was José Luís Garcia, one of more than a dozen that he used—alias Alberto Aiza, alias Felix Neri, alias Victor Nyllev....

But the FBI had only recently zeroed in on the name Ernesto Ruiz Ayala, tracking it to Tegucigalpa, Honduras, and *Servicio De Manera Clara*, an agency that offered private legal assistance for foreign nationals, asylum seekers, refugees, and adoptions.

McDade reviewed the latest reports out of Honduras. It was early in the investigation. No overt move had yet been made on the agency by Honduran police, who'd kept their surveillance covert.

There was no trace of Ayala.

On the surface, all services at the agency appeared to be legal, so police had nothing yet to support warrants, charges, or arrests.

Working with Honduran police and drawing on support from the FBI, and law enforcement from other countries, an undercover operation was recently launched. The objective was to get inside *Servicio De Manera Clara*, and gather intel and evidence that would lead to the children and Ayala.

"Ready, Jill?" Special Agent Cal Banner said. "We've got something."

McDade collected her tablet, notebook, and phone, and went with Banner, joining other investigators in the room down the hall for a hastily called meeting.

"Let's get to it." Banner made a quick survey of the room. "Ernesto Ruiz Ayala has been located in Guatemala City."

A soft cheer rippled around the table.

With his laptop linked to the flat screen at the end of the room, Banner tapped the keyboard. The big screen displayed the photos Cristina Yaqui had taken of the man at the house in Zone 15, and then the images of him and Wanda Stroud from LAX security.

"Our legal attaché in Guatemala City has received a critical lead, placing Ernesto Ruiz Ayala in the city operating a childcare center."

Banner then displayed the photos Yaqui had taken of children in the yard at the house. He outlined how the anonymous lead came in response to the FBI's Interpol notice for the subject using various aliases, and how Ayala was tied to the house.

"All of this is unfolding now. A lot of high-level geopolitical pressure is being exerted," Banner said. "Guatemala's National Central Bureau is working on getting the warrants needed to launch an arrest-and-rescue operation. The Guatemalans plan to go full throttle on this to demonstrate cooperation with the U.S. and other countries. Our sources tell us Ayala may be protected by elements within law enforcement. We expect more information soon. Meanwhile, in Honduras, we have an update on the undercover work."

Banner then showed photos of the small shopping plaza in Tegucigalpa and the storefront *Servicio De Manera Clara*. The Hondurans, with help from the FBI and others, had agents posing as couples seeking services, including adoption services.

"Not a lot of progress to report there," Banner said. "Here is a gallery of photos taken covertly of their international clients."

He flipped through images of couples in the waiting area of *Servicio De Manera Clara*. This was new, McDade thought, as she studied photos of the couples.

McDade caught her breath.

Ray Wyatt.

She glanced round the table, and then back at the photo just as Banner clicked to another.

How did Wyatt get onto this so fast? My God, he's in deep. So deep he could interfere with all of the operational work. He could bring it all crashing down. And I'm the one who tipped him.

CHAPTER 50

Tegucigalpa, Honduras

The next morning, Wyatt paced at the preboarding gate to Toncontín International Airport.

Roha was on her phone, talking softly, updating Chase Lockner, their editor in New York.

Wyatt continued pacing, watching jets and small planes taxi and take off. His thoughts returned to Gabriela Diaz's advice from the previous night.

First, Diaz had convinced Wyatt and Roha to leave their vigil of the Becks at the Diamond Sky Plaza and return to their Marriott, where she met them and updated them with her strategy.

"Do not get on the same flight as the Becks tomorrow," Diaz had said. "It would be disastrous. Fly to Guatemala City in advance of them."

"What if they cancel or change plans?" Wyatt said. "We'll lose them."

"I have reached out for help. I have sources at the Diamond, and people here who will watch them."

"So," Roha said, "when we get to Guatemala, what do you advise, since we don't know their destination?"

"I have some friends in Guatemala, but it will be tricky," Diaz said. "You have the Becks' flight number and arrival time. Keep in touch with me. Follow the Becks in a taxi. The taxis at Guatemala's airport are radio-dispatched. I have friends with the taxi service there, so when you have a lock on the Becks' vehicle, give it to me, and ensure your driver—and I hope you get a good one—is aware of your need to pursue the Becks. We both can help keep eyes on them."

It was good advice.

So, Roha booked them an early morning flight, and they checked out of the Marriott to pursue the Becks in Guatemala City.

Now, the public address crackled with a preboarding announcement as Roha stood next to him.

"Chase," she said, extending her phone.

He took it, and said, "Hey."

"Ray, how you holding up?"

"Good."

"Great work. That you've gotten this far is amazing."

"We're not done yet."

"Listen, these people are killers. Ray, please be careful."

"We know."

"What's your plan?"

"Find my son, rescue him. Then alert police to rescue other children, and make arrests. There will be a story to tell."

A moment passed, followed by another boarding announcement.

"I think that's us," Wyatt said.

"Keep me posted, Ray."

CHAPTER 51

Guatemala City, Guatemala

Ernesto Ruiz Ayala looked into the mirror.
A good face, he thought.

Thick, wavy, white hair; arched eyebrows, to accentuate the fine lines that gave him character. At 52, he still carried the charisma and confidence earned from a life of calculated risk and immense reward.

Ernesto Ruiz Ayala.
One of the identities he was currently employing.
But not for long.

He loaned over the sink in the bathroom of his big house in Zone 15 and splashed water on his face. Rivulets webbed down his skin. He grinned at the memory of how he'd used his charm to convince that silly American woman he was a screenwriter working on a movie.

Unfortunate for her that she hadn't minded her own business on their flight.

Foolish of me to have been so sloppy with my work on the plane.

He looked hard at the deepening creases around his eyes, evidence his carelessness had taken a toll. He'd lost a measure of his self-assurance after the misadventure in Los Angeles.

We took every precaution to eliminate the problem, but we were rushed.

The authorities could be coming.

He glanced at the bed and his half-packed suitcase.

His worry had necessitated the need to reevaluate his operation, expedite the process, accelerate transactions, clear inventory, and pull out.

Besides, he'd done well here in the past years, earning $75 million in U.S. dollars, deposited in banks around the world. He'd converted several million into cryptocurrency.

His underground adoption network of corrupt lawyers, counterfeiters, corrupt social services, health workers, corrupt security, hunters, and other players needed no advertising.

Word of its services floated on the dark web.

He started with Guatemalan babies, obtaining them from impoverished women in the mountain villages and city slums, convincing them to sell their children, or telling them after they'd given birth that their child had died.

While babies secured a high price, not everyone wanted an infant. Some clients were looking for children of specific genders or ages, even as old as nine or 10.

To meet that specific demand, he relied on "hunters" around the world, contracted to act on opportunity to ensure a good supply of valuable inventory. The people he used were skilled, and over the years they'd had some remarkable successes. Among them was the boy from São Paulo, Brazil; the girl from Texas; the boy from London; the girl from Spain; and the boy, to be processed in a few hours, obtained by an extraordinary hunter during a hotel fire in the Canadian Rockies.

He'd pay the hunters a generous bounty and draw upon his connections with document forgers, cartels, coyotes—all who were expert and experienced at delivering the stock to him, to enhance his inventory and be added to his catalog.

Physically, he fronted his operation with legitimate childcare and adoption services, using a "hide-in-plain-sight" strategy while paying off high-level police officials to thwart any attempt to infiltrate it.

But his worry increased with each day since he'd returned from Los Angeles. Online, he studied news reports of Wanda Stroud's case. Her body had been discovered faster than he'd expected. While most reports indicated police had no leads, he knew LAX had security cameras everywhere.

His worry evolved into fear with each new call he received from Isabel at the Tegucigalpa office. Recently, more strangers were appearing at *Servicio De Manera Clara*—strangers who said they were interested in adoption, people that made Isabel suspicious. The most recent was an American couple, claiming to be writers, one from New York and the other from Los Angeles.

"I have a sense they're journalists," Isabel said.

A journalist from Los Angeles. A journalist from New York.

He splashed more water on his face.

Stay calm.

They were winding down operations quickly.

We'll be gone within hours.

CHAPTER 52

Guatemala City, Guatemala

The one-hour flight in an Airbus A319 from Tegucigalpa was a smooth one.

Wyatt and Roha cleared Guatemalan Immigration and Customs easily. But when they checked the Arrivals board, Wyatt's stomach tensed. The arrival status for Flight EZ5716 from TGU—the Becks' flight—was delayed one hour.

Wyatt cursed.

"Hang on, Ray," Roha said as they went to seats in the waiting area. "You stay here with our bags. I'll check with the airline at the desk."

"I'll text Gabriela," Wyatt said.

Within in two minutes, Diaz responded, texting confirmation her people had seen the Becks boarding Flight EZ5716. Then Roha returned.

"It was mechanical, an unsecure latch. Fixed already," Roha said. "Their flight will only be thirty minutes late."

Biting his bottom lip, Wyatt nodded.

Still jittery, he left Roha to check the situation concerning taxis, rental cars, limo services, and shuttles. He wanted to get a sense of things, given they didn't know how, or where, the Becks would travel after landing.

"Well?" Roha asked when he returned.

"Pretty much like any other airport."

In the time they waited, Wyatt and Roha continually monitored their phones for messages from Diaz, or responses from their sources on Ayala. Nothing came. Then Roha went to the stores at the terminal's far end.

Minutes passed.

Wyatt noticed the arrival time was nearing when Roha returned with bags, opening one with fruit and yogurt cups.

"Eat something," she said.

As he spooned fruit, Roha showed him her other purchases: A wide-brimmed sun hat and sunglasses for her; a baseball cap and sunglasses for him. He smiled.

"I know," she said. "Like a bad rom-com movie, but I figured we needed something. We don't want them to recognize us."

Wyatt agreed.

As she pulled off price tags, he nodded to the board.

Flight EZ5716 from TGU had arrived.

Soon the Becks would clear Immigration and Customs, and proceed through the same walkway as Roha and Wyatt had a few hours earlier. They finished eating, disposed of their containers, put on their hats, glasses, and remained seated. They were studying a travel brochure, but eyeing the walkway when Wyatt's phone vibrated.

The number was blocked.

He answered.

"This is McDade."

A moment passed before he said, "Hi, Jill."

"Ray, I have some critical questions, and I need the truth."

"What's going on?"

"I need the truth, and I need it now. Are you in Honduras?"

Wyatt hesitated, eyeing the walkway.

"Ray, where are you right now?" McDade asked.

"Guatemala City."

McDade cursed under her breath.

"You were in Honduras, weren't you, Ray?"

"Yes."

"What're you doing?"

"I'm going to find my son."

"Listen, Ray, you're jeopardizing everything. I shouldn't tell you this, but—" she cursed again "—we're running a major operation with the PNC in Guatemala City. As we speak, they're moving to execute warrants."

"Where?"

"I'm not telling you. Ray, I know it's hard, but you have to stand down, keep out of the way. Leave it with us."

Roha nudged him. The Becks emerged with other arriving passengers in the walkway.

"I have to go."

"Ray?"

Locking onto the Becks, Wyatt and Roha gathered their bags, walked down the terminal, casually getting behind them, nearing them as they stepped outside to the taxi booth to wait their turn for a taxi.

After maneuvering and sidestepping that bordered on being rude, Roha and Wyatt got in line behind the Becks, but kept half-turned while watching the German couple get into a white taxi, #599.

Seconds later, another white taxi, #164, pulled up for them. To save time, Roha and Wyatt declined use of the trunk, keeping their bags on the floor in the back. Roha launched into rapid Spanish, telling the driver they must follow #599.

Roha and Wyatt's driver was about 50, with dark hair and glasses. He wore a blue, short-sleeved shirt. When Roha placed two American twenties on the seat beside him, he nodded, adjusting his grip on the wheel.

They eased from the airport onto Avenida Las Americas, the driver expertly and neatly weaving through the dual lanes of traffic until taxi #599 appeared a few car lengths ahead of them.

The immediate lines of vehicles came to a stop at a traffic light, and Roha got on the phone to Diaz, relaying all the information, acknowledging their taxi had a radio, and then confirming with their driver, Antonio, that #599 had one, too.

Soon, they were following it onto CA-1, a multilane expressway, part of the Central American highway system that ran through Guatemala City. The metro area—with its billboards, commercial buildings, apartment complexes, and residential section—flew by. Wyatt was somewhat relieved that Antonio was good at keeping pace with the Becks.

Traffic was heavy, but they remained close to #599. The expressway twisted and climbed as they came to Vista Hermosa in Zone 15, with its modern architecture, shops, and upscale feel.

Eventually, the taxi left the retail section for roads that curved and climbed into the hillside neighborhoods of spectacular homes, spaced apart on large properties, each one protected by metal security gates and privacy walls crowned with razor wire. From time to time, #599 would vanish around a curve in the road, making Wyatt fearful they could lose the Becks at any moment if they were to enter one of the properties unseen.

Suddenly, Antonio pulled their taxi to the shoulder and stopped.

Wyatt couldn't believe it. "What the —?"

To his horror, taxi #599 disappeared around a curve.

Roha questioned Antonio in Spanish, and he nodded to his rearview mirror.

Approaching like a silent storm from behind, emergency lights flashing, but no sirens, was a convoy of police and military trucks. Two or three dozen paramilitary personnel—in SWAT gear, riding in the back of the trucks, gripping guns—rushed past them.

Antonio spoke in Spanish.

"It's the law to pull over for police," Roha said to Wyatt.

Watching them roar by, Wyatt feared they'd lost the Becks.

A low-flying helicopter thundered above them, moving in the same direction.

CHAPTER 53

Guatemala City, Guatemala

Cristina Yaqui had made a lunch of chicken, cheese, and tortillas for the gardener and herself.

But she ate alone in the kitchen alcove and had nearly finished, while Santiago's plate sat across from her untouched.

No sign of the old man. Strange, because he'd told her he was coming in for lunch at the usual time.

As Cristina ate, her thoughts shifted, and the worry in her heart for Samuel weighed on her. She'd heard nothing from Ceto or Detective Cruz after passing along the pictures she'd taken at the house down the road. The cars, even taxis, kept coming and going.

What more can I do?

At that instant, she halted chewing her last bite. In the corner of her eye, she noticed a shadow blurring past a back window. Uncertain what it was, she dismissed it as a bird.

Then she heard a distant rumbling.

Is that thunder? It must have spooked the bird.

Taking her plate to the sink to wash it, she glanced out the back windows for Santiago. Perhaps he got absorbed in his work and forgot about his lunch? That's when she heard a shout from outside.

What's that?

Maybe the *señor* and the *señora* were in the yard instructing Santiago, or he was helping the children with something. Everyone was home today.

A bad feeling coiled around Cristina.

Wiping her hands on a dish towel, she went outside to investigate.

No one was by the pool.

Cristina hurried around to the front yard and froze.

Two men in dark clothes, with balaclavas exposing only their eyes, stood, pointing guns down at Santiago, who lay on his stomach, his wrinkled hands shaking above his head.

Other heavily armed men, with PNC and Interpol in white letters on their backs, moved in commando fashion across the property; others jumped out of trucks that growled up the driveway.

Police.

Suddenly, more shouting, cursed orders. The front doors to the house were flung open, and the *señor* and the *señora*, along with their son and daughter, hands raised, guns pointed at them, were hustled to the front yard and forced to the ground alongside Santiago.

At that instant, Cristina was thrust forward by a force that winded her, the dish towel flying from her hands. She turned, seeing a dark-clad armed commando shoving her, cursing at her to hurry toward the others.

Cristina was forced to her knees, and then to her stomach at gunpoint alongside the others. The *señora* was sobbing.

The commandos yanked at everyone's arms, pulling them back and handcuffing their wrists.

"What is this?" the *señor* asked. "This is a mistake!"

"Shut up and listen!" a masked officer yelled. "We have a judge's warrant. Where are the children?"

"What?" the senor said. "They're here beside us."

"You lie!" The officer waved to the commandos, shouting, "Search every inch of the house and grounds until we find them!"

Then a helicopter thundered above them.
Cristina's heart nearly burst.
Had she been betrayed?

CHAPTER 54

Guatemala City, Guatemala

Once the police convoy had passed, Antonio resumed driving.

After traveling a fraction of mile along the road, twisting through the enclave of stunning properties, they were halted by a police line.

A few cars of traffic were already stopped ahead of them.

Taxi #599 was nowhere in sight.

Wyatt slammed his fist down on the taxi's headrest.

Armed officers in SWAT gear stood in front of the police trucks parked across the road. No one was permitted to pass. Beyond the roadblock, Wyatt saw the gated entrance to the house where the police tactical units had converged, and his mind raced.

Could this be related to the FBI's pursuit of Ayala?

He looked around at the houses in the area. All were half-hidden behind privacy walls, security gates, and terraced properties sheltered by shrubs and palms. Again, he checked the few cars stopped ahead of them.

"I don't see #599, Sabrena. We lost the Becks."

Roha looked ahead and behind.

Minute by minute, time swept by, pushing Wyatt's heart into his stomach. He cursed.

"I think Danny's in that house behind the line!"

CHAPTER 55

Guatemala City, Guatemala

Ernesto Ayala and a few of his remaining staff were waiting at the house when the Becks arrived to pick up Luca.

"Delighted to see you again." Ayala hugged them, kissing Hanna. "And we have this young man, ready for you."

Luca emerged in the courtyard with a backpack filled with his belongings, nodding as Ayala lowered himself and spoke softly to him in Spanish.

Hanna recorded the moment, fighting her tears, passing her phone to Deiter, who continued filming as she took Luca into her arms.

"It's happened," she said. "It's finally happened. You're ours."

After a year of anxious waiting, all contracts were signed, all payments completed. Today's final step was seamless and quick.

"We'll miss you, Luca," Ayala said, "but today you start a new life, a new adventure with Hanna and Deiter."

"Thank you, Ernesto." Deiter shook his hand.

Hanna hugged Ayala just as a police helicopter pounded the sky in yet another pass, with the Becks glancing up at it.

"They're so close. What are they doing?" Deiter asked.

Ayala grinned. "The neighborhood got a notice last week that they're shooting a movie, or a TV program," he lied.

"It seems real," Hanna said, keeping her hands on Luca's shoulders.

Ayala turned to one of his staff, who passed him a manila envelope. He handed it to Deiter.

"This is your agenda, directions for your driver, and all your documentation. Everything you need," Ayala said. "Safe travels."

The Becks got back into their taxi with Luca, who waved at the staff as it pulled away.

Slowly, they passed through the gate to get on the road. Everyone in the taxi glanced left at the stopped traffic, the roadblock, and police activity.

Their taxi turned right, getting onto the clear, traffic-free side of the road to resume traveling out of the zone and to the Becks' next destination.

CHAPTER 56

Guatemala City, Guatemala

"We just can't sit here."

From his seat in the taxi, Wyatt searched ahead, craning his neck, feeling trapped, with time ticking.

They had to be coming up on 20 minutes now.

"We've lost the Becks. We're doing nothing parked here."

Wyatt had few options.

He considered calling McDade. This had to be the Guatemalan-FBI operation she was talking about. He wanted access. He deserved access. Emotion burned at the toll exacted—the price he'd paid—to reach this point.

Losing Danny.

Losing Lisa.

And now, now, down that road, I'm this close to my son!

Wyatt's anger bubbled to the surface.

"I'm getting out." He reached for the door handle. "Up there, with all the activity, it has to be the house where the Becks went, where Danny is."

"Ray, no," Sabrena said. "We need to wait."

Wyatt got out.

Roha said something to Antonio, then hurried beside Wyatt.

"Ray. They could arrest you. Let's wait to sort this out."

"Danny's in there!"

Two SWAT team members at the roadblock, watching Wyatt, shouted commands at him.

"Ray," Roha translated. "They'll shoot if you don't get back in the taxi!"

"Ask if we can speak with a commanding officer," Wyatt said.

Before Roha could say or do anything, the SWAT members shouted again and lowered their weapons.

Ahead, behind the police, at the gate, Wyatt glimpsed people in handcuffs. Was that Ayala and his people? It didn't look like him.

At the roadblock, the SWAT members shouted again at Wyatt.

Roha told the officers they were complying, grabbed Wyatt's arm, pulling at him to go back.

In the moment, Roha and Wyatt turned, they saw the gate to a neighboring house behind them, unaffected and clear of any police activity.

Taxi #599 exited, traveling away from them.

"Oh my God, Ray! It's them."

In that split second, Wyatt saw the Becks and glimpsed a child in the back seat with them.

Danny.

CHAPTER 57

Guatemala City, Guatemala

Deiter's Spanish was stronger than Hanna's, so while he directed their driver, Hugo, on where they needed to go, she was on her phone sending an urgent message, which included the new video with Luca.

While waiting for a response, Hanna stroked Luca's hair as their taxi moved down along the curving roads in the hillside neighborhood of Zone 15. Deiter smiled at the boy while watching the scenery roll by. But his smile weakened as he retreated to his thoughts.

"Aren't you pleased?" Hanna said. "We did it."

"We've invested and borrowed to pay Ayala two hundred thousand American dollars. We've taken an extreme risk. What if it doesn't work?"

Hanna sighed.

"We have Luca, right here. He is ours." She kissed the top of the boy's head. "We've analyzed the situation. Trust me," Hanna said.

Her tablet rang with a video call.

"Hello, Hanna?"

Tamina's face filled the screen.

"Tamina," Hanna said. "I'm so sorry it's late in Paris. Forgive us, but we have wonderful news to discuss with you. Did you see the video of Luca I just sent you?"

"I did. Congratulations. *He's* a beautiful boy."

"He is, and he's right here." Hanna tilted her tablet. "Wave and say hello to Tamina."

Luca waved. "*Hola*, Tamina."

Hanna watched Tamina's reaction, watched Tamina studying Luca, intently examining his features, until her smile broadened and tears came to her eyes. A long moment passed, then Tamina said, "*Hola*, Luca."

"Tamina, we found Luca through our network, a very exclusive and effective network."

"I can see that." She smiled. "Luca's a real angel."

"He's your angel, Tamina."

"Excuse me. I don't understand?"

"We searched everywhere for you, to find a boy like Rasul."

Tamina swallowed hard, staring at Luca.

"What're you saying?" Tamina asked.

"Does he not look like your son?"

Tamina continued staring. Tears rolled down her face, and she brushed them away and nodded.

"We will bring him to you to see for yourself. We'll be in Paris within 48 hours."

Tamina said nothing.

"Would you like to meet Luca?"

"Yes."

"If you agree to our administration and finder's fee, and wish to proceed, we can help you arrange for adoption from us."

Tamina's expression tightened upon realizing what was happening. She said nothing.

"Of course, if you choose to decline, we understand."

Several long moments passed.

"What are your fees?"

"Six million euros, half deposited in advance and half upon completion of all transactions when Luca becomes your son."

Tamina grimaced.

Then she reached for a framed photo of Rasul she kept nearby.

"I agree."

"Good. I told you never to give up. Miracles happen. We'll exchange details in an encrypted message. Luca, say *adios* to Tamina."

Luca waved. "*Adios.*"

"We'll see you soon in Paris," Hanna said, ending the call.

Deiter shook his head.

"I told you," Hanna said.

As their taxi accelerated on an expressway, Hanna stroked Luca's hair.

"We're going to ride on a plane, sweetheart," she told him. "Won't that be fun?"

CHAPTER 58

Guatemala City, Guatemala

Wyatt and Roha hurried back to their taxi.

"Follow them!" Roha told their driver, pointing to #599 as it disappeared around a curve.

Antonio wheeled their taxi from the traffic stopped at the police line, making a 180-degree turn, and pursued the taxi with the Becks.

"Don't lose them, Antonio!" Roha said.

Wyatt placed more U.S. twenties on his console. Antonio nodded, accelerating their taxi, and they caught sight of #599, descending the hillside community. As their taxi moved along the road, curling past properties with security gates, trees and shrubs, Wyatt shook his head.

"I don't understand what happened back there," he said.

"Your source told you there was a police operation against Ayala," Roha said.

"Yes, and that had to be it. But why did the Becks leave with Danny free and clear from a house nearby? I don't get it."

Soon they were following the taxi north on Vista Hermosa, but it was gaining distance in the traffic. Roha leaned forward in her seat, telling Antonio to not let them out of sight. They threaded west across the city, splitting

Zone 9 and Zone 10, snaking through traffic, #599 coming in and out of view.

Then #599 got onto CA-9, the Transoceanic Highway—a fast-moving, multilane freeway bisecting the country and the city. They were headed southwest; traffic was heavy. For a few miles, Antonio did well, weaving in and out, keeping close to #599. But then brake lights began to glow in all lanes. Traffic tightened and slowed to a crawl.

Up ahead, #599 changed lanes several times. Large trucks and buses obscured their view of it, as it advanced in the logjam, putting distance and vehicles between them.

Then they saw flashing emergency lights; a tractor trailer had jackknifed and overturned, blocking lanes and creating a choke point. Police were funneling traffic from several lanes to one. More than a dozen cars ahead, #599 disappeared around the wreck, just as a bus cut off Antonio, bringing their solid lane of traffic to a stop.

"We've lost them," Wyatt cursed.

"Hang on, Ray." Roha got on her phone to Diaz, and after a quick conversation, spoke quickly in Spanish to Antonio. Horns blared as he did his best to cut ahead around the bus, to get free around the wreck. But they were mired. After Roha spoke to him, he nodded, reached for his microphone and spoke to his dispatcher.

"Most drivers have personal phones," Roha said. "Diaz suggested Antonio ask his dispatcher for the phone number of the driver now on duty in #599. Then Antonio can call him."

A few moments later, Antonio's phone rang. He spoke briefly. Then, while driving closer to the wreck, he pressed his phone to his ear and began speaking again.

A few seconds later, he shared his conversation with Roha.

"Turns out, he knows the guy now driving #599. I guess they played soccer together as kids. His name is Hugo," Roha told Wyatt.

Antonio nodded. "*Sí.* Hugo."

Roha said, "He asked Hugo if he wanted to meet for something to eat after his next fare. Then in a friendly way, he asked where Hugo's next fare was ending and maybe they could meet him there. So, we have a destination. It's Villa Nueva, southwest of the city near the lake."

"The lake?"

"Lake Amatitlán," Roha said.

Wyatt took a moment, then said, "Good. *Bueno.*"

At that point, they cleared the accident. Antonio accelerated on the freeway, with Wyatt and Roha searching for #599.

As they rolled southwest, Wyatt was relieved that Antonio knew where the Becks were heading. *Why a lake?* But he remained uneasy about not having them in sight. And the puzzling events in Zone 15 gnawed at him. Staring at his phone, he contemplated calling McDade, but decided against it.

We made it this far on our own. I'm so close. I feel it.

He swiped to his favorite photos of Lisa and Danny, drawing strength from them.

Wyatt estimated they'd gone about 10 miles before they left the expressway for the city of Villa Nueva. In the distant hills, they saw the Pacaya volcano. After a series of turns through the city, they passed the Mayan Golf Club, took an exit off a roundabout, continuing to Calle Amatitlan.

But no sign of #599.

No sign of any taxi.

A motorcycle raced around them, disappearing along the road ahead.

Wyatt grew nervous, and Roha pressed Antonio to confirm Hugo had taken this route because they saw no other taxis.

"*Sí, sí,*" Antonio said.

Slightly elevated, Calle Amatitlan ran parallel to the lakeshore, in a narrow, paved roadway. Nearly canopied with lush forest growth and palms, it wound alongside the privacy walls and gates of the cottages and villas dotting the waterfront. Only their rooftops and satellite dishes were visible.

They rounded a curve.

Roha gasped.

Wyatt caught his breath.

On the right, taxi #599 was parked in front of a locked gate at one of the properties—a fortress protected by high gray-and-beige stone privacy walls, all of it topped with razor wire.

Antonio parked behind the taxi. They got out. The yowls of angry dogs spilled over from the other side of the gate. The driver, Hugo, was alone in his taxi, talking on his phone, preparing to turn and leave. He stopped when they stood in front of his car.

After a quick conversation with Antonio and Roha, Hugo confirmed that he'd just dropped off a man, a woman, and a boy from Zone 15.

Wyatt looked for an intercom, or bell, on the gate to call. That prompted Hugo to warn them in Spanish.

"Ray," Roha said. "Hugo said the dogs are dangerous. Vicious. And there are private security guards with guns inside."

Wyatt climbed to the roof of Antonio's taxi and looked over the gate.

The dogs growled.

Through the razor wire, he saw a building, then a cluster of smaller buildings—probably a boathouse. In the gaps, where the property sloped to meet the water, a long dock extended out over the lake. On land, at the dock's start, he saw the Becks, with Danny. They were talking to a man who appeared to be examining their documents. Another man standing nearby appeared to be waiting to take their bags to the end of the dock and load them onto a waiting seaplane.

"They're getting ready to fly out!" Wyatt said to the others.

"Fly out?" Roha said.

"On a seaplane!"

With the high razor-wired walls surrounding the property, the dogs, and armed guards, there was no chance Wyatt could climb over the wall and run down to the dock. Farther down the shore, where it curved around a small cove, Wyatt surveyed neighboring cottages.

A large motorboat was docked at one nearby.

He hopped down.

"We have one chance to stop them. Get in the car. Let's go!"

CHAPTER 59

Guatemala

Jack Clay and Leon Palma came up from the dock heading for Clay's Jeep.

"It's a beautiful boat, Jack."

Clay had shown his friend, Palma, a Guatemalan Army colonel, his new SuperXT Glider, a 27-foot motorboat with twin inboard engines.

"We love it," said Clay, a former U.S. Marine Corps lieutenant colonel from Virginia. "It's the icing on our retired life here. Been three years now."

"I told you when I was in Washington, you'd love this place."

"It's been a dream, my friend," Clay said as they got into his Jeep.

The men were going to the Mayan Golf Club to join their wives.

"Yes, it's been a dream." Clay repeated. "Except for the Morales place up the road."

"What about it?"

"The widow sold it, almost two years ago now. Looks like the people who bought it turned it into a vacation rental. Now with that floatplane you saw, flying in and out all the time, I don't know what's truly going on. I mean, it's likely legitimate, but I don't know."

"It could also be a front for smugglers, or cartels," Palma said. "I could make some calls, Jack. See what I can find out."

"Sure." Clay shrugged. "But I got protection in the house, the boat."

"Berettas?"

Clay nodded. "And a couple of ARs. We're good. Lately, some of the owners were thinking of hiring private security, too. Like everybody else."

He eased the Jeep up to his gate and pressed the remote control on his visor. The steel gate automatically opened.

"What the f—?" Clay said.

A taxi wheeled up to block the entrance.

Wyatt and Roha got out waving their arms, Roha pleading in Spanish for help.

Clay nodded for Palma to open the glove box and remove his gun as a precaution, while he ordered Roha and Wyatt to keep their distance.

"Stop. Just keep your hands where I can see them," Clay said.

Quickly, Roha explained that they were American journalists pursuing an illegal child-abduction network; that at this moment, a child-smuggling operation involving foreign nationals was taking place up the road; that an escape by seaplane was imminent; and that they needed help with a boat now.

"Because the child is his son!" Roha pleaded.

Clay asked for Roha and Wyatt's identification while Palma kept the Beretta close. They showed IDs for True Signal News, and their driver's licenses.

After a moment of quiet discussion between Clay and Palma, two veteran soldiers, Clay switched off the Jeep's motor and closed the gate.

"Damn! Gives us a story to tell our wives," Clay said. "Let's get to the boat."

As the four of them trotted to the dock, with Roha telling Palma more details, Palma took out his phone and made emergency calls. All of them got into the motorboat. Wyatt and Roha untied the ropes. Clay started the SuperXT Glider; its twin engines grumbled to life, and they eased away from the dock.

Clay then pushed the throttle forward, the bow rose, and the 500-horsepower craft sliced through the water directly toward the seaplane, less than a quarter mile away. As they approached, their view of the plane's dock improved. They saw a child, a man, and a woman board the seaplane, saw the doors close. Seconds later, the plane's single engine started and someone at the dock cast off the tie ropes.

As the boat got nearer, Clay passed a key to Palma, pointing to storage areas where he kept two ARs and ammo.

"Get them ready, Leon. Just in case!"

It may have been because the plane's pilot spotted the boat, but the plane began taxiing and gaining speed to lift off.

"We won't make it! We can't stop them to talk!" Clay shouted over the engines and the wind to Wyatt and Roha.

"Stop it from taking off!" Wyatt said. "Whatever it takes!"

Clay glanced toward his guns, which Palma had readied, and kept his boat on a collision course with the plane.

"Everybody hang on to something. Now!"

Clay turned the boat sharply half a football field in front of the plane, peeling a massive curtain of water from the surface while carving a deep wake. To counter it, the pilot throttled the plane. But the huge wake early during takeoff forced the plane to prematurely become airborne, lift roughly from the water, and then slam down, teetering. One of the wings sliced into the water and broke off, twisting and flipping the plane. The prop churned water until the engine stalled.

Turning the boat, Clay headed to the crash, slowing as they came upon the wreckage. The cockpit was upside down, submerged and slowly sinking. Pulling alongside, Wyatt and Palma jumped into the water.

Gulping air, swimming below the surface, they worked on opening the doors. They glimpsed Hanna struggling upside down in her seat belt. The pilot and Deiter were unconscious; so was the boy.

The impact had crumpled the fuselage, making it difficult to open the doors. Palma and Wyatt surfaced. Clay passed them a claw hammer from his toolbox and a large knife.

Palma and Wyatt submerged. Using the hammer and pulling, they got the doors open. Palma cut the seat belts with the knife. The angle and seating meant first Hanna swam free, pulling Deiter behind her to the surface, while Palma grabbed the pilot.

Last, alone and unconscious, was the boy.

Danny.

Wyatt was out of air; his lungs were bursting.

Suddenly, the cockpit began shifting and sinking.

His ears pulsing, his heart drumming, he summoned every degree of his strength. He could hear Lisa's voice as he swam down, reached into the cockpit, seized Danny's arm, and pulled.

I lost you once. I won't lose you again.

Kicking, stroking, Wyatt ascended to the light, breaking the water's surface. Gasping, swallowing air, he immediately began giving Danny mouth-to-mouth resuscitation, as the others pulled them onto the boat. Wyatt continued CPR and mouth-to-mouth until Danny coughed, spit out water, and opened his eyes.

Wyatt took Danny into his arms.

Roha shrouded them with a towel, embracing them.

Palma held Hanna at gunpoint, as she watched over Deiter and the pilot, who also coughed up water, while Clay guided his boat to his dock.

Along the shoreline, they saw the flashing lights of the police.

Wyatt held his son the whole time, never letting go.

CHAPTER 60

In Guatemala City, about the time Wyatt and Roha's taxi had left the hillside community to pursue the Becks, the police action on the house of Cristina Yaqui's employers was proving fruitless.

The search had yielded no evidence of a childcare center, let alone an illegal adoption network.

"You're making a big mistake! I want to call my lawyer!" the *señor*, handcuffed with his family and Cristina, continued calling out to officers.

"Please, you have the wrong house!" the *señora* shouted, while comforting her handcuffed children.

Cristina clenched her eyes shut, convinced the raid was retaliation for her attempt to help her nephew, for which she would go to prison.

The family's protests and the unsuccessful search prompted commanders of the PNC and Interpol teams to double-check the information on the warrant. To their horror, their respective copies differed, giving them two different addresses. Calls were made to confirm that the correct address of their target was, in fact, linked to the property a short distance down the road.

Urgent commands were issued over radios, but by the time they shifted the operation to the correct address, Ernesto Ruiz Ayala, was gone.

The property was empty.

Children's toys, food, and clothing were everywhere—clear evidence of a childcare center and front for an adoption network.

A check with the police helicopter patrolling overhead showed its video camera had captured a vehicle departing the Ayala property moments earlier. A replay of the recording enabled police to get a visual on the fleeing vehicle, strong enough to track it and issue an alert.

Moments later, on Vista Hermosa, patrol cars surrounded and blocked the SUV in a dramatic stop. Ernesto Ruiz Ayala—the subject of an Interpol Red Notice, a global fugitive, wanted for murder and other charges—was pulled out at gunpoint, arrested, and handcuffed.

***

Miles away at Lake Amatitlán, German nationals Hanna and Deiter Beck had survived their plane crash in their failed attempt to flee the country illegally with a trafficked child. They faced numerous charges after the initial police investigation showed they had planned to fly to Belize City, then to Miami, and on to Europe.

Using counterfeit documents and helped by corrupt officials bribed by Ayala's network, the Becks conspired to deliver the child to an individual in Paris, where they would offer the child for "adoption" in exchange for a large payment.

Further investigation, aided by authorities in Munich, Germany, showed the Becks were planning to repeat their enterprise by targeting wealthy individuals around the world who were grieving the loss of a child.

In Paris, when French police arrived at Tamina's home, she was waiting with three powerful attorneys, ready to defend her position that she had no idea of, and no connection to, any criminal activities by the Becks.

For his part, Ayala faced extradition to the United States, where he would stand trial for the murder of Wanda Stroud, and a range of other human-trafficking charges, supported by the investigations of law enforcement in several countries.

Ayala's house in Zone 15, and his administrative office, *Servicio De Manera Clara*, in Tegucigalpa,

Honduras, underwent processing by local teams, supported by FBI evidence experts.

Their work yielded records that helped McDade at the FBI, along with police around the world, arrest a number of key players in Ayala's network. Among them was the man who ultimately confessed to abducting Danny during the chaos of the hotel fire in Banff, Alberta, and fleeing Canada with him.

The records also helped locate other children stolen by Ayala's network and ultimately reunite them with their true families in São Paulo, London, Madrid, San Antonio, and many other cities.

Investigations also led to the arrests of ranking immigration officials, attorneys, and law enforcement officials in Belize, Mexico, Honduras, Panama, Brazil, the U.S., and Europe, including many police officers in Guatemala City who were above Detective Sebastian Cruz.

***

In the time that followed, Guatemala's interior minister, who oversaw the PNC, issued an apology for the botched raid on the house of Cristina Yaqui's employers.

In the flow of media reports on the story, the role Cristina Yaqui had played emerged. She soon became a hero on social media. Cruz and the public defender, Karen Ceto, praised her. So did the FBI in Los Angeles, who supported editorials and calls for the U.S. government to offer to bring Cristina and her nephew to the United States—in gratitude for her courage, and to escape any risk of retribution in Guatemala.

Ceto was successful in getting the court to give Samuel Yaqui a three-month suspended sentence for his crime, which passed quickly after the time served, starting with his arrest, was included.

In the U.S., nonprofit groups helped Cristina find a home and a job, helped Samuel with school, and both of them with a path to citizenship.

***

In California, Colleen Eden led the drive to have a memorial plaque honoring Wanda Stroud placed in the flower bed at a park near her home in Downey.

Wanda's neighbors and friends raised close to $100,000 to start a foundation in Wanda's name, dedicated to protecting children around the world.

***

McDade returned to Manhattan to follow up on any remaining tentacles of the Hydra case, while working on her other investigations out of the FBI's New York headquarters.

Whenever they could, McDade and her daughter, Alison, would go out to Queens to visit Ray Wyatt, Danny, and Molly.

***

In the immediate aftermath of the rescue, Guatemalan police and social welfare officials had taken custody of Danny Wyatt.

With the help of the U.S. Embassy, a required DNA test was done, proving Wyatt was Danny's father. At the same time, embassy officials, working with their counterparts in Guatemala, Washington, D.C., and New York, arranged for all official documentation to be expedited.

It allowed Wyatt to return to the U.S. with his son as soon as possible.

At that time, Wyatt turned down interview requests from U.S. news outlets and media around the world to focus on helping his son recover.

At home in Queens, Wyatt ensured Danny underwent several medical exams. Doctors determined that while Danny had no physical injuries and no indications of abuse, he had suffered severe psychological trauma.

Dr. Irina Kostoff, a psychiatrist specializing in treating children who've survived abductions, had a number of initial sessions with Danny, aided by a Spanish-speaking psychologist who could translate.

"As you know, Ray—" Kostoff removed her glasses "—Danny's endured overwhelming upheaval from being abducted in the fire at age three, taken from the world and parents he knew."

Consequently, Kostoff explained, Danny had lost his self-awareness at the critical stage of his young life.

"You are a stranger to him, Ray. He identifies as Luca, and lost the English that he had known."

Kostoff stressed how it would take time to win Danny's trust, and securely return him to his interrupted life.

"He's suffered a type of psychological amputation, and he's likely to have nightmares, outbursts, panic attacks. All of it is a normal response. It's going to take patience and love to help him heal."

"I can do that," Wyatt said, noting that he was already working on improving his Spanish.

Kostoff arranged to have regular sessions with Danny. She then suggested things Wyatt could do to help, which included introducing Danny as a nickname, eventually using it more than Luca. She suggested allowing Danny to see any of his mother Lisa's things, "maybe draw a scent from any of her personal belongings you may have." Kostoff also suggested showing Danny recordings of the family together.

"Of course, there's Molly," Kostoff smiled. "While she may have been a pup at the time, she'll remember Danny, and her affection will help with his healing."

Kostoff approved of Wyatt inviting Sabrena Roha to move into his home in Queens, where they would work on the exclusive series of stories on Ayala's adoption network for True Signal News.

"More important than the story," Kostoff said, "Sabrena will help him recover. She was with you in Guatemala. Her presence, her ability to speak Spanish, will comfort and assure him. She can help him with English, be a bridge to your relationship with him."

Later, at home in Queens, during a quiet moment, Roha told Wyatt that the death of her fiancé, Cliff, had left a gaping hole in her heart. Now, having lived through the anguish of Guatemala with Wyatt and Danny, she'd found a new measure of meaning in her life.

Wyatt invited Roha to consider staying longer after the story was done, maybe even ask Chase Lockner for a transfer to New York.

That's when Molly put her head on Roha's lap.

As the days passed, during Wyatt's private, dark moments, he realized that a part of Danny was stolen, gone forever. But at times when he, Danny, and Roha would take Molly for walks to the park near the house, Wyatt saw something new was growing.

One afternoon, Wyatt steeled himself and drove alone, south of his home in Rego Park, to a cemetery along the Jackie Robinson Parkway. He walked along the tranquil lawn to a bench under a tree near the headstone for his wife. He sat in silence for a long time before speaking.

"I found him Lisa. I brought him home."

Wyatt covered his face with his hands.

"When he's ready, I'll bring him here."

A soft breeze caressed him, and birdsong celebrated the day.

That night at home, when Wyatt looked in on Danny asleep in his bed, he noticed that Danny was gripping the moose figurine in his hand.

AUTHOR'S NOTE

I hope you enjoyed *Requiem*, which features Ray Wyatt. Ray is featured in three books. Along with *Requiem*, he appears in *Into the Fire*, and *The Hollow Place*. The Ray Wyatt series is loosely drawn upon my experiences as a reporter. If you liked *Requiem*, I hope you will consider following Ray in the other stories.

In bringing this story to you, I benefitted from the hard work and support of a lot of people.

My thanks to my wife Barbara and to Wendy Dudley for their invaluable help improving the tale.

Thanks Laura and Michael.

And a very special thanks to Tracy Turner and Jackie Olson for going above and beyond.

I want to thank readers. For without you, a book remains an untold tale. Thank you for setting your life on pause and taking the journey. I deeply appreciate my audience around the world and those who've been with me since the beginning who keep in touch. Thank you all for your very kind words. I hope you enjoyed the ride and will check out my earlier books while watching for my next one.

Feel free to send me a note. I enjoy hearing from you. While it may take some time, I try to personally respond to all messages.

Rick Mofina

https://www.rickmofina.com/
https://www.instagram.com/rickmofina/
http://twitter.com/RickMofina
http://www.facebook.com/rickmofina

ABOUT THE AUTHOR

Photo credit: Michael Mofina

Rick Mofina is a former journalist who has interviewed murderers on death row, flown over Los Angeles with the LAPD and patrolled with the Royal Canadian Mounted Police near the Arctic. He has also reported from the Caribbean, Africa, Kuwait and Qatar. He has written more than 30 crime fiction thrillers that have been published in nearly 30 countries. He is a two-time winner of Canada's Arthur Ellis Award; a Barry Award winner, a four-time Thriller Award finalist and a two-time Shamus Award finalist. Library Journal calls him "One of the best thriller writers in the business."

For more information, please visit:
https://www.rickmofina.com/.

Made in United States
North Haven, CT
15 May 2023